## "The clock i[illegible]
## know how m[illegible]
## Bu[illegible]



"Before I get pulled back, you've got to figure out how to override it all and send me back farther, back *before* The Prophet took over my body. He said I made a mistake that led to this. Which means I have to go back and stop myself from making that mistake; I have to pick the right moment."

Willow pressed a hand to her forehead. "Which is?"

The Slayer lowered her gaze and a shadow fell across her face. "I don't know. What could I have done differently? I want you to use your magick to give me a chance to find out."

"I wish I had as much faith in me as you do," Willow said with a soft laugh. "I'm going to get on the research right away."

"Good. While we're waiting around for that, we can work on the plan."

"Plan?"

"Take Sunnydale back and kill Giles."

"Ah." Willow nodded. "That plan."

**Buffy the Vampire Slayer™**

Buffy the Vampire Slayer
(movie tie-in)
The Harvest
Halloween Rain
Coyote Moon
Night of the Living Rerun
Blooded
Visitors
Unnatural Selection
The Power of Persuasion
Deep Water
Here Be Monsters
Ghoul Trouble
Doomsday Deck

The Angel Chronicles, Vol. 1
The Angel Chronicles, Vol. 2
The Angel Chronicles, Vol. 3
The Xander Years, Vol. 1
The Xander Years, Vol. 2
The Willow Files, Vol. 1
The Willow Files, Vol. 2
How I Survived My Summer Vacation,
Vol. 1
The Faith Trials, Vol.1
Tales of the Slayer, Vol.1

The Lost Slayer serial novel
Part 1: Prophecies
Part 2: Dark Times
Part 3: King of the Dead
Part 4: Original Sins

Available from ARCHWAY Paperbacks and Pocket Pulse

Child of the Hunt
Return to Chaos
The Gatekeeper Trilogy
Book 1: Out of the Madhouse
Book 2: Ghost Roads
Book 3: Sons of Entropy
Obsidian Fate
Immortal
Sins of the Father
Resurrecting Ravana
Prime Evil

The Evil That Men Do
Paleo
Spike and Dru: Pretty Maids
All in a Row
Revenant
The Book of Fours
The Unseen Trilogy (Buffy/Angel)
Book 1: The Burning
Book 2: Door to Alternity
Book 3: Long Way Home

The Watcher's Guide, Vol. 1: The Official Companion to the Hit Show
The Watcher's Guide, Vol. 2: The Official Companion to the Hit Show
The Postcards
The Essential Angel
The Sunnydale High Yearbook
Pop Quiz: Buffy the Vampire Slayer
The Monster Book
The Script Book, Season One, Vol. 1
The Script Book, Season One, Vol. 2

Available from POCKET BOOKS

# THE LOST SLAYER

## Part Three

## King of the Dead

**CHRISTOPHER GOLDEN**

An original novel based on the hit TV series
created by Joss Whedon

POCKET PULSE
New York London Toronto Sydney Singapore

For information regarding special discounts for bulk purchases, please contact Simon & Schuster Special Sales at 1-800-456-6798 or business@simonandschuster.com

**Historian's Note:** This serial story takes place at the beginning of *Buffy*'s fourth season.



An *Original* Publication of POCKET BOOKS

POCKET PULSE, published by
Pocket Books, a division of Simon & Schuster, Inc.
1230 Avenue of the Americas, New York, NY 10020



ISBN: 0-7434-1187-0

First Pocket Pulse printing October 2001

10 9 8 7 6 5 4 3 2 1

POCKET PULSE and colophon are registered trademarks of Simon & Schuster, Inc.

Printed in the U.S.A.

# Previously on Buffy the Vampire Slayer . . .

*A new breed of vampire arrived in Sunnydale, faster and stronger than others of their kind, and with a kind of magickal energy surging inside them. These are the Kakchiquels, vampire servants of the ancient Mayan demon-god called Camazotz.*

*Buffy had recently come to believe that the only way she could be content in her life and still be an effective Slayer was to separate the two halves of her life completely, as though Buffy and the Slayer were two distinct people. That meant trying her best to keep her friends out of her life as the Slayer, to handle those duties all by herself. But having the best of both worlds soon proved more difficult than she had expected.*

*Even as she began to learn more about Camazotz and the Kakchiquels, and to attempt to locate the demon-god's lair in Sunnydale, Buffy was visited by the ghost of former Slayer Lucy Hanover, who brought a warning. An entity of the spirit realm, a clairvoyant being called The Prophet, had predicted that Buffy would soon make a mistake that would have catastrophic results.*

*Before she could follow up on Lucy's warning, the search for Camazotz heated up when it was determined that his current lair was probably a ship moored on Sunnydale's coast. Despite Buffy's desire to handle it on her own, Giles insisted that it would be faster to have Willow use magick to locate Camazotz and that they would attack as a group, given the gravity of the threat represented by the Kakchiquels and their master.*

*Buffy was supposed to have Willow gather the ingredients necessary for the spell and then the two of them were to meet Giles in Docktown, the run-down section of Sunnydale where the town's shipping industry is concentrated. But when Buffy called Oz's looking for Willow, the young witch was not available. Though she left part of the message, Buffy chose not to tell Oz about the spell, the ingredients, or the planned rendezvous, hoping Willow's absence would cause Giles to abandon the search for the night. She planned then to search for Camazotz on her own.*

*But Giles was not deterred. Over her protests, Giles and Buffy went together to the harbormaster's office, hoping to discover some hint of strange goings-on that might indicate which ship Camazotz was using as a lair. Giles insisted she stay in the car.*

*The harbormaster turned out to be a vampire in service to Camazotz. While Giles waited and Buffy grew impatient in the car, the harbormaster informed the demon-god of their arrival. Buffy realized things had gone wrong and broke into the harbormaster's office to find her former Watcher in the clutches of that vampire. Then Camazotz and a group of his Kakchiquels appeared, and the Slayer was faced with a terrible choice. If she fought, Giles would probably be killed. If she surrendered, they would both likely die. Knowing that the first rule of slaying is to stay alive, and reasoning that Camazotz would keep Giles alive to use as bait to lure her, she fled the scene.*

*Later, as she and her friends tried to determine the location of Camazotz's lair, now desperate to rescue Giles before it was too late, Willow summoned the ghost of Lucy Hanover. The spirit indicated that The Prophet's visions had grown stronger. Fearing that The Prophet's dire predictions may have something to do with her current predicament, Buffy asked Lucy to see if The Prophet would speak to her. When the dark, sinister apparition known as The Prophet did appear, she revealed that Buffy had already made the mistake and that the dark future she had predicted could not be averted. She offered to let Buffy see this future, which she claimed she could do if Buffy let her into her mind.*

*But The Prophet was not what she seemed. In truth, she was Zotzilaha, the estranged bride of Camazotz, fleeing from her mate in spirit form and searching for a powerful host body with which to defend herself against her husband. Zotzilaha had come to Sunnydale to possess the body of the Slayer, and Camazotz had come in pursuit of his errant bride.*

*When Zotzilaha touched Buffy, she invaded the*

*Slayer's body and forced Buffy's soul out. Through magick whose nature has yet to be revealed, Zotzilaha pushed Buffy's soul forward in time five years, into the nightmare future about which she had warned the Slayer.*

*The soul of Buffy-at-nineteen was merged with the soul of her older, future self. In that dark future, Buffy found herself in captivity. Years before, the Kakchiquels had captured her and chosen not to kill her so as to avoid the rise of a new Slayer.*

*Buffy eventually escaped and found that vampires now controlled all of Sunnydale and its surrounding environs, their influence spreading with every passing day. She made her way south out of Sunnydale, where she linked up with representatives of the Council of Watchers. The Council has set up a base and a large force of operatives whose mission it is to thwart the reign of the vampire king she has heard rumors about. Among those operatives are her old friends, Willow, Xander, and Oz, all of whom have been changed by the hard years since they last saw Buffy.*

*Willow then revealed the most horrifying truth of all about this terrible future.*

*The king of the vampires is Rupert Giles.*

# CHAPTER 1

D*rusilla's dead.*

Spike roared through downtown Sunnydale in a silver Camaro with blacked-out windows. Dawn had come hours ago, and the sun glared down upon the windshield, streamed in through the small splotches that had not been painted black. He had to see to drive, after all.

Behind the black aviator sunglasses he wore to keep the sun off his eyes, tears streaked his face. His jaw was clenched tight, his knuckles white on the steering wheel. Though he would usually have something on the radio, all was silent in the car. No music. Not even the sound of breathing. Not from him, for after all, wasn't he a dead man?

Yes, of course he was. Yet somehow he had never felt quite so dead as he did this awful morning.

*The Slayer. That little bitch.*

But it had not been only the Slayer's fault, had it? No,

not at all. When Giles had split them up, sending Dru with one team and him with another, he ought to have balked, but he did not. Giles was the king, wasn't he? He hadn't steered them wrong yet.

Till now. Now he'd steered them all kinds of wrong.

*Bastard.*

There were big plans. Spike wanted to be a part of it. But now Drusilla was dead and everything they had worked for with Giles was in jeopardy. For millennia, vampires had dreamed big but acted small, never able to agree on anything long enough to get it together, to pull off a scheme bigger than a simple slaughter. Rupert Giles was different. Using the addictive blood of the bat-god, Camazotz, to ensure loyalty among the Kakchiquels, he wanted nothing less than the world. Unlike so many vampires and demons, he had achieved the level of patience that immortality afforded him. What he had in mind would take time to do right. He would wait.

*But now this thing with the Slayer. What the hell is this all about?*

Images of Drusilla sifted like kaleidoscope images through his mind. He could hear her mad little laugh, remember what she looked like naked and spattered with blood, recall the scent of her, like freshly pressed antique lace with just a hint of lilac.

Fresh tears sprang to his eyes and he let them stripe his cheeks like war paint. They dripped onto his black leather jacket and he let them dry there, a sort of offering to the ghost of his dead love.

If only vampires had ghosts.

Spike drove out of downtown, haunted as an empty circus tent, awaiting the mad revelry that night always brought. The Kakchiquels kept the residents of Sunnydale about for their own amusement. Blood slaves. Sex slaves. Torture victims. Yet for every human they killed, two more would drift into town on the current of whispered gossip and the desire to discover the truth, to subject themselves to the rule of the vampires. These humans would do anything to be tasted, to be bled, to have a Kakchiquel lover, and if having their guts strewn across the sidewalk downtown or their heads rammed onto a fence post at the edge of Hammersmith Park was a moment by moment possibility, that was a small price to pay.

Then there were the original Sunnydale residents, the people who hadn't had the courage to run away. Most of them cowered in their homes, even now, or operated their businesses with the permission of the dead who slept while the sun was high. Those were the ones Spike understood the least and disliked the most.

*Cowards.*

In silence, he drove to City Hall. It was warm inside the car and though it didn't really bother him, there was something wrong with that today. His chest felt hollow, as if a slender surgical blade had somehow been slipped into him and his heart carved out, cold and dead but still saturated with other people's blood. With Drusilla's death, he had become a shell of himself, a mask with no face beneath it.

*How can it be warm?*

Spike was certain that he ought to feel cold, and so he turned the air conditioner up as high as it would go and relished the stiffness in his fingers as his body temperature began to dip even lower.

Spike pulled into the underground garage beneath City Hall and parked in the spot reserved for him. He was ice now, a brittle, hollow sculpture of frozen pain shaped like a man. At some point his tears had stopped and now as he stepped out of the car, jacket cascading behind him, there was only his grief to mark Drusilla's passing.

From a pocket inside his jacket he pulled out a white plastic key card. At the door that led into the complex he slid the card into a slot and a light burned green. The door clicked and he pushed it open and entered the warren of corridors beneath City Hall. There were tunnels from there that would lead to the basement of the courthouse, the police station, even the town library.

Spike clutched the key card and strode along one of those tunnels, the scrunch of leather the only sound to accompany him. At a junction in the corridor, he turned left and walked to a bank of elevators, where his key card was needed to call an elevator down.

He stepped in and pressed the button for the third floor, then waited as the elevator glided upward. In the corner there was a security camera. Spike was a shadow of himself, a kind of ghost in his own right, and as he glared at the security camera from behind his dark sunglasses, he wondered if the guards in the monitor booth could see the change in him. He wondered if they saw him coming, and shuddered.

He hoped that they did.

The elevator *shushed* to a halt and the doors slid open. A pair of burly Kakchiquels stood blocking his exit, their eyes crackling with energy, their tattooed faces impassive. Spike was not at all surprised to see them.

"You are not expected until dusk," one of the Kakchiquels said, voice emotionless.

"The master does not need you until then," added the other.

Spike cocked his head to one side, regarding them through the tinted glasses. He slipped his key card into his pocket. The elevator doors began to close and he punched the button to open them again.

"Yeah. He mentioned that. Wanted me to take a little time, cool off a bit, right?" Spike nodded, but then stopped abruptly. "Bugger that."

With one swift motion he reached out, grabbed the one on the left by a clump of hair, and hauled him forward, driving his knee up into the Kakchiquel's crotch. The vampire doubled over and Spike yanked him into the elevator, then stepped off. The other Kakchiquel was ready for him, or at least thought he was. Spike took one blow to the temple that knocked his sunglasses spinning through the air, then grabbed the vampire by the face and squeezed, breaking his jaw and fracturing his cheekbones. He knew his own eyes flickered with the blazing power of Camazotz, just as his enemy's did.

With a low snarl, Spike rammed the vampire back

against the wall, then grabbed his hair in a tight fist and shoved the guard's head through the emergency glass covering a fire extinguisher. Broken glass sliced his hand but Spike barely felt it as he snapped the heavy fire extinguisher from its moorings and began slamming it into the Kakchiquel's skull until it was mashed to pulp and splintered bone.

The guard dusted.

A ding sounded behind him and Spike turned to see the elevator doors opening again, the guard he'd kneed standing inside. With a twist of his arm, he swung the extinguisher again and shattered the guard's nose. Spike struck him again and again, beating him down, then pressed all the numbers on the elevator before stepping off. The elevator moved down, taking the bloody, crippled Kakchiquel with it.

Spike did not smile. He no longer had anything to smile about. No one with whom to share the exhilaration of a good fight, a good kill. Instead he picked up the black glasses from the floor and slipped them back on. He reached into his coat, took out a box of cigarettes and a metal lighter, and fired one up.

He strode down the hall and around a corner that led him to the huge double doors of the courtroom. There another pair of Kakchiquels were standing guard, and they snapped instantly to attention, ready to stop him.

Spike took a drag on the cigarette, blew out the air, and gazed at them coolly from behind his shades, where he hid the telltale spark of power that bound him to these other creatures.

"I know, I know," he said. "You're supposed to stop me, yeah? Bloody hell, mates, have at it then. But think about it this way. Mood I'm in right now, you'll have to kill me to stop me. If you can. And if you do, well, he's gonna miss me, isn't he? Then he'll kill you blokes sure as I'm standing here. His lordship is fickle like that. On the other hand, you stand aside and he'll punish you, sure, but you'll live."

Spike took a long drag on the cigarette, blew rings of smoke into the air and barely even glanced at the two Kakchiquels as they exchanged a nervous glance. After a moment, they actually opened the large double doors for him.

He winked at the larger one and went into the courtroom.

The rows of seats were filled with vampires, eyes crackling with orange fire, black bats seared into the tender flesh of their faces. Spike found that there were fewer and fewer familiar faces as the months went by. Giles sent those he trusted out on errands of vital importance. They were part of the plan. But he had always kept Spike and Drusilla close at hand, either because he felt he needed them or because he didn't trust them, or both.

The lights were dim in the huge room and the only noise was the shifting of the Kakchiquels in their seats as Spike entered. They were a motley collection of vampires, from those who had been servants of Camazotz when the bat-god had come to Sunnydale, to existing vampires like Spike himself who had been recruited by Giles, to new creatures made only recently.

Giles sat on the dais—where the judge would have presided, if there were any judges left in Sunnydale. His eyes glowed only very dimly. His graying hair was combed neatly back and a soft, benevolent smile turned up the corners of his mouth. He wore a thin green V-neck sweater with a white tee shirt underneath. To those who had known him as a human being, only the fact that his glasses were missing would have shattered the illusion that he had not changed at all.

Brilliant, kindhearted, self-effacing. That had been Giles the man, the Watcher. It was a face he wore still, though no one knew what sort of pleasure he derived from the façade.

Of all the vampires in the chamber, only one other besides Spike was standing. He was a dark-skinned leech whose ritual tattoo had been seared into his face with white ink instead of black. The bat-scar was the color of milk and it set him apart from all the others. Giles called him Jax. Spike did not know if he had any other name. He had simply appeared one day, a creature sired by Giles and then suckled by Camazotz as was their tradition. But Jax had quickly become far more than simply another recruit. He was Giles's right hand.

Spike hated him.

Jax glanced once at Spike, a small smile flickering across his features, then he gestured at a female vampire in the front row.

"Valerie? I believe your report is next."

"I don't think so," Spike snapped as he strode up the aisle toward the judge's bench.

Hushed mutterings filled the room.

"Spike. You're half a day early. You have a private audience scheduled at dusk today."

"Bollocks," Spike replied happily.

He walked right up to Jax. No one tried to stop him. Jax moved to block his way, hate simmering in the other vampire's gaze. Spike took another drag on his cigarette, plucked the butt from his mouth between two fingers, and pressed its burning, ashen end into the middle of Jax's forehead. The leech snarled in pain and anger, his features contorting into the bestial face of the vampire.

Spike decked him.

He stood before the bench and glared up at Giles, whose eyebrows shot up with curiosity Spike found insulting.

"She's dead," Spike said, voice a rasp. "You might as well have struck a match to her yourself, you bastard. What are you playing at with this Slayer? You could've had her a dozen times since she got out."

For a moment, just the tiniest flicker, the mask slipped. A shadow of menace seemed to fall across Giles's features. The smile gave way to a lip-curling snarl. His nostrils flared and the orange fire in his eyes became tiny embers. Then it passed and the kindly, almost paternal smile returned to his features.

Giles leaned toward him and gazed down from the judge's bench. "Go. Sit. Valerie is next. When she's done, we'll talk about what went wrong last night, and what we've all lost."

As though Spike had suddenly disappeared from the

room, Giles gestured for Valerie to come forward. Jax rubbed at the burned spot on the white brand on his face, but he, too, gave his attention to the Kakchiquel girl. It infuriated Spike to be ignored like that, but he supposed it beat having Giles order a room filled with vampires to kill him. Still, Spike did not sit as Giles had instructed. He might take orders from the big boss, the king, but he was still his own man. He had a legend of his own to maintain. Giles knew that . . . he constantly used Spike's status as an object of fear to his advantage.

Jax might be the master's right-hand man, but Spike was his enforcer, his assassin. *At least when Drusilla was alive. Now, though . . . Giles has a lot to answer for.*

Valerie, one of those whom Giles had trusted and promoted, glanced uneasily at Spike as she stood. He flashed the girl a grin born from his savage heart and she flinched and looked quickly away. Valerie moved forward and stood beside Jax, staring up at Giles in total subservience. She even bowed.

"Lord and master," Valerie said, her voice sweet and yet confident. "The Los Angeles operation proceeds as per your charted strategy. LAPD sirings are at twenty-two percent. Complete departmental takeover is scheduled for next Wednesday, with the mayor and the commissioner twenty-four hours previous."

Giles stroked his chin thoughtfully, his gaze distant. Half a minute ticked by and no one dared interrupt his thoughts.

"Oh, all right, you pompous git. Get on with it," Spike snapped. He rolled his eyes and crossed his arms, feeling self-conscious there at the front of the courtroom.

He expected a flare of anger, but Giles did not so much as blink. Valerie glanced at Jax, then shifted uncomfortably from one foot to the other. Jax seemed unwilling to even acknowledge there was something odd about the master's behavior. After another half minute ticked by, though, he moved into Giles's field of vision.

"My lord?" Jax ventured.

"Hmm?" Giles muttered. Then he glanced down at Spike and Valerie and blinked several times. "Oh, right. Sorry. Late night, wasn't it?"

Valerie giggled like a schoolgirl and Spike wanted to rip her heart out for it. The king was getting a bit dotty. They all had to see it. Ever since Buffy had broken out of her cell, Giles had been scattered. Never mind that he'd turned up missing from his chambers half a dozen times, not telling anyone where he'd gone.

"Valerie, I don't believe you mentioned the studio heads," Giles reminded her.

"Last night, my lord," she replied. "Just as you instructed. We missed at Paramount, though. He took some unscheduled personal time, went to a spa in Nevada. A team has been dispatched."

"Excellent initiative." Giles stood up. The instant he did so the entire room also rose. "We'll pick this up tomorrow morning. Any urgent reports or requests can go to Jax." His smile grew wider as he looked at Spike. "In my chambers, now, William. And we'll discuss your bereavement."

Jax shot Spike a withering glance as he moved into the aisle, only to be surrounded by those Kakchiquels who felt that their business with the king could not wait. Spike caught Valerie studying him with fascination. Another time he might have flirted with her, strutted for her. But the tears were dry upon his cheeks and Drusilla's death was too fresh for him, too close.

Giles stepped down from the high chair and went to the heavy wooden door that led into the judge's chambers. He opened it and stood aside, waiting for Spike. The smile was still there, but a chill ran through Spike when he caught the glint in the other vampire's eyes. Though he remembered well when Rupert Giles was the Watcher, a stuffy Englishman who relied more on knowledge than on violence, this creature was not that man. Not a man at all. It retained Giles's memories, his intelligence and cunning, and it had turned them to its advantage.

But this king of vampires had not become lord and master to thousands by chance.

That knowledge calmed Spike somewhat as he stepped past Giles and into the darkened chambers beyond. The windows had been blacked out and the three lamps that burned in the room were unable to dispel the shadows there. In the corner, the skeleton of Judge Warren Hester had been arranged in an embrace around a coat rack. Tufts of hair and dried skin still clung to the bones. At night the windows were opened to air the rooms out, but over the years the smell had mostly dissipated.

"Hello, your honor," Giles said to the bones.

Then he turned and leaned against the desk, crossed his arms and gazed at Spike with sympathy in his glittering orange eyes. Sympathy as false, as feigned, as the benevolent mask he always wore.

"Have you got another cigarette?" Giles asked.

Spike raised one eyebrow in surprise, then shrugged and tugged the pack from his pocket. He held it out and Giles took a cigarette. Spike lit it for him, clicked the lighter closed, and slid it back into his pocket with the cigarettes.

Giles inhaled deeply, cig clutched between two fingers. Then he let it dangle in his hand as he leaned against the desk once more.

"You know how important Drusilla was to me, Spike," he said, as the ash lengthened on the cigarette. He did not take another drag from it, however, only let the ash grow longer. "Honestly, I find it more than a bit disturbing that you'd accuse me of having some sort of responsibility for her destruction. Why would I do something like that?"

Feeling more than a bit petulant, even childish, Spike glanced at the ground. "Not saying you did it on purpose, Ripper. But, look, you're playing with the girl. Me, I always thought it was brilliant, keeping Buffy locked up like that. You don't kill her, they don't get to train another one. But she got out, didn't she? Not sure it was too bright an idea puttin' that new one, the little cutie came along after I took care of Faith, in with Buffy. Gotta figure that was a mistake, but it's too late to do anything about it now. Right. Fine. But they could have caught up with Buffy five minutes after she was out the door, or any time while she was on her way to Sunnydale. You told 'em to wait. More'n that, you left her that damn crossbow."

A ghost of a grin whispered across Giles's features. "You knew about that?"

Spike shrugged. "Saw you leavin' with it, put two and two together. At the time I figured you were just toying with her, having a bit of fun all your own. I can understand that. Once upon a time, she was your girl, yeah. In a way, you were her sire the same way Angel was mine. He didn't make me, but he trained me to be what I am. You did the same for her. So maybe you play with her a bit, give the mouse a little string, but you don't let her go."

Spike took off his sunglasses, stared hard at Giles. "You don't let her run around killing your best people. Harmony was an idiot, but she was vicious. Matthias and Astrid, they were the best of the ones who came here with Camazotz. And Dru—" his voice broke off.

"I should've been there!" Spike snapped, shouting at Giles, who watched him impassively. "You had us all spread out, but I think you knew just what Buffy'd do. You trained her, after all, right? Who'd know better than you. You probably predicted every move she made. You played with her, but you gave her too much rope and now Drusilla's dead."

Giles nodded slowly, reasonably. "True," he said. "All of it. You know, you've always been underestimated, Spike. You're really far more perceptive than you get credit for."

Spike shook his head, not knowing what to say next. The last thing he had expected was that Giles would simply agree with him, taking responsibility for Drusilla's death.

The vampire lord rolled his eyes. "Oh, please, Spike!" he cried with frustration. "What would you like me to do about it? I'm sorry Dru's dead. Truly. She was always a source of great amusement. Couldn't find any better. And the occasional vision, when it wasn't too truncated by her lunacy, was helpful as well. But she's dead. So now what? You stomp around like a five-year-old and then go huffing off to Greece or Brazil to lick your wounds? Feel free, if you need to."

Spike flinched. He felt the anger boiling up inside him, dwarfing anything he had felt before. This wasn't just the pain of his loss, the void in his gut where his love for Dru had been ripped from him. It was more visceral, more personal even than that. He had spent over a hundred years proving his worth after Angelus and Darla had disparaged him. He had killed more Slayers than any other vampire he knew of. But Giles had just brushed him off as though he was worthless.

"I'll tell you what you do," Spike snarled. His face changed with his anger, his fangs lengthening, his brow contorting into the face of the beast. "You get a posse up like an old Western, as many of your loyal subjects as you can pull together on short notice, then you track her down and you kill her before she can do any more damage. Or maybe you don't remember the habit Buffy has of interfering with the fun?"

Giles's upper lip twitched once. He glanced away and idly reached up toward his face as though he were about to remove a pair of eyeglasses. His fingers paused inches from his face and he made a fist, then dropped his hand. Spike frowned as he took note of this strange behavior. It was, in that moment, as though Giles had forgotten that he no longer needed glasses. An echo of an instinctive nervous behavior that he had engaged in when he was still human. Still alive. Still really Giles.

"You don't want to kill her, do you?" Spike asked, astonished. "What's got into you, Ripper? You gone soft?"

A shudder seemed to pass through Giles. He bent over slightly, staring up at Spike from beneath heavily lidded eyes. His face changed, became monstrous, lips curled back to show his elongated fangs. Slowly, he took a step toward Spike.

"You have a certain value to me, Spike. I gave you a great deal of rope because of it. No more."

Spike tried to protest, but Giles was too fast for him. The vampire lord darted in and grabbed him by the throat. Lifted off his feet, Spike beat at Giles's head and arms, trying to break his master's grip. Giles gave him a swift head-butt, connected with a loud, solid crack, and then slammed Spike into the dead judge's desk.

"It is not your place to question!" Giles roared as he kicked Spike in the ribs once, twice, a third time.

Bones snapped.

"Somebody's gotta do it," Spike snarled, not sure if

he felt brave or just stupid. He clutched at his side and tried to rise, and Giles grabbed him by the front of his jacket and threw him hard enough that he crashed into the coat rack and the wall and sent the dead judge's skeleton clattering in pieces all over the floor.

When he looked up, Giles stood over him. The vampire lord kicked him in the face and Spike felt his cheek give way.

"Son of a bitch!" Spike grunted in pain.

Giles crouched beside him. His face was human again, his features soft, the mask back in place. Somehow that was more terrifying to Spike than anything else.

"Everything she is, she owes to me, just as though she were my own daughter. She is a more perfect creature, a more effective predator, than any of the beasts who follow me. I wanted to see that beauty, the flow and rhythm of it, again. To know that it is still there."

Spike wiped the back of his hand across his mouth and it came away bloody.

"Yeah, that's brilliant," he muttered. "Things are going too well for you, too smoothly, so you've got to muddy the water a bit. Seen it a million times. Done it myself, even. Winning's no fun if you don't have someone to beat. Doesn't mean it isn't stupid."

Giles kicked him in the gut, then bent to pick up a length of broken coat rack. He turned and strode away, as if Spike were little more than a nuisance, now almost forgotten.

"I toy with her. For my own pleasure. It isn't your

business. But if you must know, I don't intend to kill her, not really. I didn't want her to escape, but now that she's out, she'll never let herself be captured alive again. I want to see if she's still as deadly. It seems all her time in that cell has made her even more so. Buffy Summers is the perfect killer. Imagine what she could be if I turned her."

Spike's eyes widened. Painfully, clutching at his broken ribs, he climbed to his feet. "You're gonna make her a soddin' vampire?"

Giles glanced over at him and smiled sweetly. "Of course I am. Anything else would be a terrible waste, don't you think? Besides, I'm going to have to have someone to replace you."

"What—" Spike began.

He was not allowed to finish. Giles darted across the room at him, broken coat rack in his hands. It whistled as it cut the air, then collided with Spike's skull. He staggered backward, lifted his arms to try to defend himself, and Giles broke his right hand with another swing of the coat rack.

"No!" Spike roared.

"I have to set an example," Giles said simply, coldly. "If only you hadn't been so fresh."

The vampire lord jammed the coat rack into Spike's gut and propelled him with a mighty thrust back through the blacked-out windows. The painted glass shattered and Spike tumbled out into the daylight. He fell three stories, twisting himself in midair, trying to control the descent. When he struck the pavement below, he dislocated a shoulder and his broken ribs tore up his lungs. Pain erupted in him like fireworks and he blacked out for a second or two.

His clothes began to smoke and then tiny flames erupted all over his body. Spike started to burn.

His eyes popped open and he screamed in anger and agony. With some difficulty, he got to his feet and ran for the entrance to the underground parking garage.

*Self-righteous bastard,* he thought as he slipped into the cool relief of the garage, out of the sun, slapping at his clothes and hair to dousc the flames. His keys rattled in his pocket.

*Can't kill ol' Spike that easily.*

Giles had slipped into the shadows quickly enough that he was barely scorched by the sunlight that streamed in the broken window. His face and hands felt warm, but that would pass in moments. The window would have to be replaced, of course. He could have had it boarded up instead, but he thought, perhaps, that his affection for the symbolism of painting the windows over might have finally waned. No, this time he wanted a real window, with a fine wooden frame and heavy drapes to block the sun during the day. That way, should he ever have occasion to enter that chamber after dark, he could look at the stars.

Spike would probably survive, he knew. But despite his swagger, Spike had never been the most courageous of creatures. Self-preservation was always his greatest motivation. Without Drusilla to trail along behind in puppy-dog fashion, he was likely to grumble under his breath and wander off, go on an intercontinental rampage or the like, then come back in ten or fifteen years with his plumage showing, all cock of the walk.

When he did, Giles suspected he would take Spike back into the fold. By then he would appear to have been properly chastised. And he was useful, after all. His legend was more substantial than he was, but Spike was an excellent hunter, a bright boy, and a decent strategist when he set his mind to it. A bit too emotional, but then, Giles was not entirely without guilt in that area himself.

He thought of Buffy again, and smiled to himself. Never had he seen another creature so resilient, so durable. In his secret heart he had been disappointed that it had taken her so many years to escape, though she was quite a nuisance. Now that she was out, though, he rejoiced in the carnage she had caused.

Always, she had been like a daughter to him. Soon enough, she would be his daughter in truth. His blood would make it so.

Careful to avoid the sunlight, Giles went to the corner where Judge Hester's bones had been scattered, and he began to tidy up. He whistled happily while he put things back in order, thinking about the evening to come, and the brief journey he would make that night.

A journey south.

# CHAPTER 2

*In her dream, there are two of her.*

*Buffy-at-nineteen seems to float in a current of darkness that rustles her hair and clothes, pushes against her. She can feel it dragging against her from behind as well, particularly at the base of her skull, as though some unseen thing has violated her flesh, painlessly plunging a hook through the peak of her spine. It tugs on her, but the flesh and bone are uncomfortably numb.*

*Amid the darkness that sweeps by her there is a bright core, a deep purple vein that surges with electricity and menace. Now that she has noticed it, she can see that it disappears into the distance ahead of her and behind, weaving in serpentine fashion and yet following the same path as this river of darkness that pulls at her.*

*A chilly certainty shudders through her and Buffy traces the purple vein with her gaze, follows it until she realizes that it runs right up to her chest. Suddenly it is warm there, where the energy cable enters her, and she feels stronger, more aware. How she did not notice before that this power touches her, she has no idea. But she also suspects that the feeling at the base of her skull, the fishhook that is tugging her along the river of darkness . . . that feeling is there because the bruise-colored, thrumming energy stream that enters through her chest exits her body right at the top of her spine.*

This thing. This is what's pulling on me, *she thinks.*

*Yet something holds her in place, floating there. Something has anchored her here.*

*Buffy-at-nineteen glances downward. A kind of spotlight is shone in this dark place, and she sees Spartan living quarters, a hard bed, a rough blanket. Upon the bed, Buffy-at-twenty-four rests uneasily, dreaming, twisting beneath the blanket. Her features are beautiful, but hard-edged like diamonds. Her arms where they snake out from beneath the covers are corded with sinewy muscles, her fingers leathery with callus.*

Me, *she thinks.* That's me. Or it will be.

No. No, it *is* me. It shouldn't be, but it is.

*Buffy-at-nineteen blinks, and she truly sees. The purple vein snakes from her, back through the darkness, where it attaches to Buffy-at-twenty-four like some monstrous umbilical cord.*

*And she knows what it is.*

This is the power, *she thinks.* From the first Slayer to the last, this is the power of the Chosen One. *And on the heels of that thought, another.* Why is it so dark?

*"Buffy?"*

*A voice swirling in the river of darkness.*

*She turns to look back along the rushing river, the serpentine vein twisting in the flow, and she sees a face back there. For a moment it is vague and out of focus, but then the features shimmer and become clear. Waves of blond hair, a kind but tired smile. So familiar, so intimate.*

*"Mom?" Buffy asks. "Where are you?"*

*The tired smile disappears. "Here, now, honey. Just here."*

*"I need to see you," Buffy whispers. "I have to find you."*

*Joyce Summers shakes her head, even as the current begins to take her, dragging her back and away, along the river and into the void.*

*"Faith tried to save me. I thought you should know," Joyce says.*

*Buffy's eyes widen. Her heart clenches painfully in her chest. She tries to swim the current, to go after her mother as the woman begins to diminish in the distance. But she is anchored now to Buffy at twenty-four, and cannot follow.*

*Still, there is something she must know.*

*"Who?" Buffy-at-nineteen screams after the dwindling figure of her mother. There are the ghosts of tears on her cheeks. "Who killed you?"*

The tears were still wet on Buffy's cheeks when she woke. She had kicked off the covers and the sun shone through the window, casting a distorted square of warmth and light across her legs. It was too warm and she pulled her legs up in front of her, curled into an almost fetal position there on the bed. The sun felt wrong to her. Too good; too healthy; too rich with heat and life. It was as though the sun itself were unnatural, merely a hesitation between stretches of night, a gasp of brightness and false security before the dark came again.

That was what Giles had done.

*Giles,* Buffy thought. It was a joke cast down by the cruelest of gods, that her former mentor and friend should become this thing, should be transformed into the most vile example of the monsters he had fought his entire life.

In her mind's eye, Buffy could see a clear image of Giles, a kind, decent man who had been more of a father to her in her teenage years than her own father had been.

*Oh, Giles,* she thought again.

Through some dark and powerful magick, a being called The Prophet had thrust Buffy's soul five years into the future, so that she now existed inside her own twenty-four-year-old body. Twin spirits, one younger, one older, thrived within her and though their memories and thoughts were sometimes in conflict, for the most part they had merged. Buffy had reason to believe it was a temporary situation, but she resigned herself to growing accustomed to it, just in case.

In this dark future, Buffy had spent the previous five years imprisoned by the vampires, and had escaped to find that her best friend, Willow Rosenberg, had grown wiser and more powerful and was now a major player in the war against the darkness. Willow had told Buffy how it had all come to this, or at least as much as they could guess. The god of bats, Camazotz, had come to Sunnydale followed by his Kakchiquels, a breed of vampires somehow enhanced by his own demonic power. Striking out at the Slayer, Camazotz had ordered Giles made a vampire.

It was the greatest mistake the god of bats had ever made. Giles was brilliant and cunning, with an encyclopedic knowledge of demonology and a violent, dark streak he was at pains to keep hidden. Once the vampiric spirit had taken up residence in the dead man's psyche, adopting as vampires usually did the knowledge and personality traits of the victim, Camazotz had created his worst enemy. Giles established himself as king of the vampires.

What happened to Camazotz, no one really knew. But the Kakchiquels, old and new alike, still seemed to shimmer with the power of the god of bats, and so Willow and the others presumed the Mayan deity was still alive.

Yes, Willow had told Buffy all of that, and more, and it had broken the Slayer's heart. But there were a great many things Willow had not told her. She had not, for instance, said anything about the murder of Buffy's mother. Had talked around it, in fact, changing the subject at least twice to avoid it.

Only through her dream had Buffy learned the truth.

*The dream,* she thought now. *The line of the Slayer's power stretching into the future and back into the past.*

A thousand questions filled her head, but she pushed them all away. They could wait until later. Wait until she had spoken to Willow.

The night before she had been rescued by an extraction team led by the girl who had once been her best friend—the young witch nineteen-year-old Buffy *still* thought of as her best friend. Xander and Oz had been with the group as well. All of them had been different, changed by time. Hardened. Yet after an awkward first few moments, Willow had softened. Buffy thought that she had seen within this powerful witch the girl she knew so well. It felt as though they had reconnected.

But now Buffy was not certain. Her mother was dead and she felt sure that Willow had known it.

All of these thoughts weighed heavily upon her as she rose from bed. The small room she had been given had a full bathroom and though she had showered before falling asleep the night before, she did so again now. The water was hot and the steam swirled in the room. She breathed the warm air in, and it felt as though she were scouring not only her body but her lungs as well.

In the closet Buffy found some clothes that had been left for her the previous night. Nothing was her size, but that was not a surprise. It was not as though they had had much time to prepare for her arrival. She managed to find jeans, a tee shirt and a hooded navy blue sweatshirt that fit her. In the stale-smelling room, she bounced on her toes and spent a few minutes doing stretching exercises.

Somehow, she had to find a way to explain to Willow what had happened that night five years ago, to make her understand how two versions of the same mind, two moments of the same soul, could exist in one body. With Willow's help, Buffy had to find a way to separate her twenty-four-year-old body from the nineteen-year-old soul inside her, find a way to return her younger self to its rightful place.

It would happen eventually, Buffy knew that. It was already history. But she did not know how to make it happen, or even how long her younger persona was meant to stay in this hideous future.

With a leap, she balanced on the metal frame of the bed, crouched with her arms out. Then she executed a perfect backward somersault, and swept through a series of shadow-boxing jabs and kicks that shook her loose, got her blood flowing.

Somehow she would figure out how to get her split soul back to where it belonged. But for the moment, there were things that had to be attended to right here.

Five years earlier she had taken on too much, tried to force herself to live two lives at one hundred percent each. Ironic, given her current predicament. But she was only one person. Buffy Summers was the Slayer, and her life had to be broken up accordingly. That meant that she had to have help sometimes. That night, years ago, she had tried to do it all herself. Her insistence upon that had probably led to Giles's initial capture, and her efforts to free him had led to everything else.

If she had been more practical, more honest with herself, from the beginning, this future would never have come to pass.

Now that it had, however, she was not going to rest until she set things right. She had to find the lord of vampires, Rupert Giles.

And dust him.

Buffy took a last glance around the small room they had given to her, and smiled softly. Whatever her resentments, whatever her fears, this tiny room was a vast improvement over the much larger cell she had spent the past five years in. The window alone, with the sun shining through, made all the difference. More than that, however, was the simple fact that she could open the door and walk out.

Curious and almost trembling with momentum, with the desire to take action, Buffy went out into the corridor. Whatever this installation was where the Council had set up its task force—if that was what they were—it was cold and featureless, almost military. The floors were covered in gray industrial carpet, the walls painted a sort of jaundiced white that made Buffy think of old bones.

On impulse, she started off to the left. She passed an open door and saw a thirtyish guy doing pull-ups on a bar inside the room. When he spotted her walking past, he lost his focus and let go of the bar. He watched her, but Buffy glanced away. Several others passed her as she wandered, all of them in drab gray paramilitary uniforms or neatly pressed business suits.

At a junction in the corridor, she caught the scent of food off to her right. The cafeteria, she assumed, and so headed in that direction. Her stomach rumbled loudly as the thought of food drew her on.

As she approached the open double doors of the cafeteria, however, a small door opened on her left and a familiar figure emerged. Oz wore droopy denim pants and a green cotton V-neck shirt that hung loose on him. It occurred to Buffy that they both looked like they were wearing someone else's clothes.

In the moment before he saw her, Buffy studied Oz's face. His hair was longer than it had once been, swept back from his forehead in shaggy waves, and there was a reddish stubble on his chin. Though as always his expression revealed nothing of his inner emotions, there was a melancholy in his eyes that gave her pause.

Oz sniffed the air, then glanced up at her sharply.

"Buffy," he said, as if it were hello.

"Oz," she replied.

They shifted uncomfortably for a moment there in the hall, half a dozen feet from each other. Buffy broke the silence.

"I was just wandering around. Trying to orient myself."

Oz nodded once. "You want the ten-cent tour?"

"I'd like that."

For twenty minutes they walked the halls of the installation together. Though his narration on the tour consisted mostly of things like "library" and "training area," Buffy enjoyed his company. She sensed no guile in Oz at all. But there was more to it than that. As they walked down a long flight of stairs she thought would eventually lead them back to the corridor where they had met up, she paused and turned to him.

Oz arched an eyebrow.

"You trust me," she said, and it wasn't a question.

"Yeah?"

"Why?"

Though his features were fully human there was something of the wolf in the way he cocked his head just then. "Some reason I shouldn't?"

Buffy sighed. "No. It's just, last night I felt this kind of static from Xander and even from Willow. It's been a long time, I know. But this seems like more than that. Not that I'm expecting everything to be the way it was—"

"Nothing is," Oz interrupted.

"I know. I understand that," Buffy insisted. "Just feeling a little like the wicked stepsister here. I don't know if it's resentment or what, but it's like they don't want me here."

"Willow led the extraction team," Oz reminded her.

Buffy nodded, smiled awkwardly. "Yeah. Yeah, she did. Maybe I'm just wigged because it's been so long since I've seen you all. Since I've seen anyone who still had a pulse."

"Maybe," Oz replied. "Maybe not. Life went on, Buffy. Willow always believed you'd come back, but in the meantime, we've got this war. Whole big machine pretty much running on its own. My guess? It's gonna take some time to figure out where you fit into it."

Buffy understood immediately what he meant, for she had been feeling almost exactly the same things. She had to figure out what her role was supposed to be now, and so did Willow and the others on the Council. Awkwardness was inevitable. She just had to have the patience to ride it out.

Oz turned and started down the stairs again. Buffy followed him quickly and grabbed his shoulder, still intent upon speaking to him. When Oz snapped around to glare at her, there was a snarl on his face, his lips pulled back to expose his teeth. Buffy flinched and drew her hand back, and Oz's expression softened immediately.

"Sorry," she said.

"It's all right. I don't like to be touched. You didn't know."

And there it was, exactly the sort of thing that she had been thinking about seconds before. The way things were right now, she didn't fit in. She only hoped that would change.

"I guess there's a lot I don't know," Buffy replied. "How . . . how did you get control of your wolf side?"

Oz's nostrils flared. He scratched the back of his neck idly, as if she had not asked the question at all. At length he glanced at her again.

"Had a situation where it was either let the wolf out or die. So I let it out. Been working on it since."

"And it wasn't the full moon," Buffy pressed.

"No moon at all. Breakfast time, actually. Never did get to finish that cinnamon roll." The corners of Oz's mouth twitched briefly, as close to a smile as anyone was likely to get from him. "You want to know why I trust you?"

Slowly, Buffy nodded.

"We've all changed. Maybe on the face of it, so have you. But there's something in you that's just the same, like a flashback to when things weren't quite so nasty. I've got to get going. We all have responsibilities here."

Oz started down the steps away from her again. Buffy could only watch him go, turning his words over in her head.

"Welcome back to your war," he said as he reached the bottom of the steps and began to walk off.

"Wait, Oz," she called after him.

A pair of older men in suits hurried by as Buffy went down the stairs after him. They barely spared her a glance.

"Why is it my war? Why not yours, too?"

"I only stay for Willow. Not sure she notices, though."

Then Buffy understood the sadness in his eyes. Whatever was between him and Willow now, it was not what it once had been.

"Well, what about Willow?" she asked. "Why does she stay?"

Expressionless, Oz studied her for a moment. Then he inclined his head, just slightly. "She stays for you."

The cafeteria reminded her an awful lot of high school. She passed over some of the less identifiable foods and opted for a chicken Parmesan sandwich. It was not quite cold and the cheese had all but congealed on the top, but as hungry as she was, Buffy barely noticed. There were French fries as well, and those, at least, were hot.

When she turned to glance about for a place to sit, Buffy became extremely self-conscious. She caught several people staring at her, but most of them looked away the instant she noticed them. A pair of young, lean guys watched her for a few moments too long, then turned to each other and began to whisper.

Suddenly she was back at Sunnydale High again. The new girl, with a reputation that had preceded her. *Rumor has it she was booted out of her old high school in L.A. for burning down the gymnasium. What a freak.*

Buffy shook those feelings off. High school had been a long time ago, and after the years she had been without any human contact at all, even curious stares and rude whispers were better than isolation. Though she was tempted to take a seat with one of the scattered groups in the caf, she had too many questions in her head, too much on her mind to simply socialize.

In the middle of the room, she found a small round table that was empty, and sat down alone. A short time later, while she was peeling an orange she hoped would get the greasy taste of the chicken out of her mouth, Xander came into the cafeteria. Relief washed through her. She was pleased to see someone she knew, someone who was a friend, despite the grim demeanor that now seemed almost constant for him.

Though she had seen him clearly enough last night, she was not at all used to his appearance. At twenty-four, Xander barely resembled the boy she had first met back in sophomore year of high school. All the lightness, the sense of jest, had gone from his eyes. He had often worn his hair too long and unruly. Now it was shorn only a few inches off the scalp, which only served to exacerbate the severe cast to his features that was punctuated by the crescent-shaped scar on his face.

He spotted her and strode over, his gait hurried and stiff.

Xander did not sit. It pained her, that little detail. The visible changes in him seemed confirmed by this. Yet with Xander she did not take it personally. Whatever experiences had caused his personality to be altered so dramatically, this behavior was not aimed at her. This was simply who Xander was now. Once upon a time, he would have sauntered into the room and dropped himself like a particularly agreeable rag doll into the chair.

No longer.

"Willow asked me to tell you there's a debriefing in five minutes if you want to attend."

So many things she wanted to say to him, to ask him, but Xander seemed like a wall to her, and all Buffy could do was nod. "Where?"

"I'll take you," Xander replied.

When Buffy did not rise to follow him, at last he reluctantly sat down across from her. The last of the peel came off the orange and Buffy tore the fruit in two. She handed half across to him. For a moment Xander only stared at the sticky, dripping orange as if it were some foreign object. Then he took it from her.

"Thanks," he said, as he popped a piece into his mouth.

"It speaks," Buffy said, almost afraid to tease him but more afraid of not trying to break the ice between them.

To her great relief, he smiled. For just a moment, she saw the old Xander in there.

"I missed you, Xand," Buffy told him, though after all the time she had spent alone the words were hard for her. "I missed all of you."

He swallowed hard and put the rest of his orange down on the table, uneaten. Xander rose and faced her.

"We should go."

"God, what happened to you?" Buffy asked him, frustrated.

He hesitated, then shook his head. "Another time, Buffy."

When Xander led her into the conference room, Buffy was at first startled by how many people were crammed inside. Though the room had clearly been intended for smaller numbers, there were at least twenty people standing around a long wooden table. Nine others were seated around the table, at the far end of which there was one vacant seat. Buffy glanced back at Xander curiously, but he only nodded for her to proceed. He would not be sitting, apparently.

Which made her wonder exactly how one earned the privilege of a chair. Willow was seated at the table, dressed in a brown suit that was quite flattering on her. It made her look even older than she was and reminded Buffy that this was not the teenager who had been her best friend. A buzz of conversation filled the room as Buffy looked around at the others at the table. At the end, opposite the empty chair that had been left for her, sat a sixtyish woman with her hair in a tight bun and her hands folded primly on the table in front of her. Her eyes had a ferocity in them that was anything but prim. To her left was a large man in paramilitary garb whose nose had clearly been broken several times. It was flattened and skewed to one side. He had the look of an old-time boxer, but beyond that his most prominent feature was that his hands were enormous. Buffy did not think she had ever seen a human with such large hands.

They made him look dangerous, even monstrous.

The biggest surprise for her was on the other side of the older woman, however. There sat an Asian girl with pink hair pulled back with barrettes. She could not have been more than fifteen. The girl met her gaze and some indefinable connection was established between the two of them, a sort of primal recognition. Even if she had not felt that, she would have known why the girl was present. Why else would they have a girl that age at a gathering like this?

*The Slayer,* Buffy thought. *The one replacing August.*

It gave her a shock to see the girl, to remember the other recent Slayer, whom she had accidentally killed.

And beside the new girl, the only other familiar face in the room. He had grown a neatly groomed beard and there was some gray at his temples now, but Buffy would have recognized him anywhere.

"Wesley?" she said, surprised to find herself pleased by his presence.

"Hello, Buffy," he replied, not without warmth. "Why don't you have a seat so we might begin?"

The older woman at the head of the table cleared her throat. "Or, rather, conclude, as the case may be," she said as she gazed at Buffy. "Miss Summers, my name is Ellen Haversham, and I am the director of the Council's operations here in California. To my left," she said, motioning toward the man with the pugilistic features, "is Christopher Lonergan, my chief of staff and tactician. To my right, Anna Kuei, the current Slayer."

Buffy furrowed her brow deeply.

"Oh, my apologies," Ms. Haversham said, almost amused with her slip. "I meant other than yourself, of course."

Buffy wanted to punch her.

"Of course you already know the present Watcher, Mr. Wyndam-Pryce, and our sorcerer, Miss Rosenberg."

Willow looked up and smiled and Buffy felt a moment of relief. Maybe things weren't as strained as she had thought after last night.

"We have a great many questions for you, of course—"

"You do, huh?" Buffy asked, a bit incredulous.

"Buffy—" Willow warned.

"'Cause, gotta say, I have a big batch of questions for you guys, too." Buffy shouldered through those gathered around the table until she reached the long windows on the other side of the room. She opened them all, and fresh air began to circulate.

"A little stuffy in here, I thought," she explained, and glanced pointedly at Ms. Haversham.

Then she walked over to the empty chair, ignored it, and perched on the edge of the table. Though there was a great deal she needed to talk about, she wasn't about to do it in front of all these people.

"I've been in a cell for five years," Buffy said, her eyes on Ms. Haversham and no one else. "Not that I don't appreciate the assist last night, but I think maybe before you get to debrief me, I should at least be able to get answers to a few simple questions."

Ms. Haversham's face took on a decidedly sour expression. Then, to Buffy's surprise, the older woman fidgeted slightly, and then glanced down the table to Willow, as though seeking permission. It took Buffy a second to realize that everyone in the room was watching Willow, and then she knew that the real power in the place did not sit at the head of the table.

"What about it, Will?" Buffy prodded.

Willow nodded, but she was not smiling. "Whatever makes you the most comfortable."

"Fine," Buffy said. "Why didn't you tell me my mother was dead?"

Out of the corner of her eye, Buffy saw Xander reach up to touch the scar on his face. She turned toward him but he only stared back at her, so Buffy returned her attention to Willow.

"How did you know?" the witch asked, her expression softening.

"I had a dream."

Willow nodded.

"Why didn't you say anything?" Buffy asked, and in

her own voice she could hear a plaintive tone that she did not like. It was an appeal not to the room but to the woman who had once been her best friend.

For just a moment, Willow glanced away. Then she met Buffy's gaze and sat a bit straighter in her chair. "I didn't tell you," she said, voice steady, "because we were there and we didn't save her."

Despite the strength in her voice, there was pain and sadness in Willow's eyes, in the set of her mouth. In that moment Buffy felt as though they were communicating not across the room but across the years they had been apart. Emotion charged the air between them; sorrow at what they had all been through. Yet there was something else there as well. Whether it was simply her own sense of guilt, her own mind at work, Buffy could not say, but she felt certain that in Willow's eyes she saw disappointment and a troubling question. *Why weren't you here?*

"It was a long time ago, only four or five weeks after you were captured," Willow went on, "but it cost us a lot."

Willow's gaze ticked toward Xander and then back to Buffy.

"What's a lot?" Buffy asked, intuiting that the conversation was painful for her friends, but not able in that moment to let concern for their pain supplant her own. Somehow she had to fill the hollow place within her created by this confirmation of her mother's death, and yet she knew that was something she could never do.

"Your mother," Willow replied. "The scar on Xander's face. And Anya. If it hadn't been for Oz, we'd *all* have died that day."

*Had a situation where it was either let the wolf out or die,* Buffy thought, remembering Oz's words.

"Anya . . ." Buffy said, almost to herself.

She looked over at Xander. He met her gaze without wavering, no expression at all on his face. Whatever he had seen that day his girlfriend died, Buffy thought it had killed something in him, like deadening the nerves in his soul.

"Who?" Buffy asked Willow, her voice cracking. "Who killed them?"

"It was Spike," Xander answered from amid the crowded room. "Giles gave the order, but it was Spike who did it."

Twice in the previous two days, Buffy had been close enough to Spike to kill him and had not been able to do so. A shudder went through her now and she clenched her right hand into a fist at her side. For a moment, all she could do was breathe. Then she stared at Willow again.

It was as though everyone else in the room had disappeared, and it was just the two of them, trying to make sense of what the world had become, what they had become.

"Angel?" Buffy asked, dread filling her. "If he was alive he would have come after me, right? When did he die?"

"We don't know that he did," Willow told her, her tone regretful but unwavering. "I called him the day you were captured. He came the same night, went out looking for you, and never came back. As far as we know, Giles never said anything about it to anyone, at least not in earshot of Faith, or any of our spies in Sunnydale."

Buffy felt sick. *Faith.* Just another on a long list of people she cared about who had died because she wasn't there to save them. She had a thousand other questions but did not think she had the energy for them. Grieving, she at last slipped into the leather chair and leaned forward to gaze at Willow.

"What is all this?" she asked. "The Council was never this militant."

"We never had to be," the big man, Lonergan, intoned.

His voice destroyed the illusion that this was a conversation between old friends. Buffy wished it really were just the two of them, but she understood that was not how things were done with the Council. It never had been, really, and now Willow was one of them, if not actually a member of the Council, at least working with them.

Reluctantly, she turned her attention to Lonergan.

"We never had to deal with an infestation like this before," the man continued. "Leeches generally keep to themselves, but this group's different, yeah? More powerful, more organized, and Giles at the top of it all."

"We've got the full cooperation of the U.S. government," Willow added. "The military influence is theirs. After Giles and the Kakchiquels started taking over Sunnydale, we found out that, hey, surprise, the government had been running a kind of monster research facility right there in Sunnydale. All roads lead to the Hellmouth."

"You're kidding," Buffy said.

Willow's dubious expression told her all she needed to know.

"They had to pull the plug on their project when the Kakchiquels killed the entire staff on site. The people running that show couldn't get more funding. They were supposed to be primarily a research group, not a combat unit, which was what was needed. That's where the Council came in. I had contacted Quentin Travers when Angel didn't come back, but by then Wesley was here. The rest is sort of history. The federal government doesn't want the rest of America to know what's going on, so they've helped fund the Council operations. They've provided special forces training, weapons, and a jurisdictional freedom not even the DEA has, as long as we help them pretend there isn't a thirty-mile-square block of southern California enslaved to vampires.

"Of course, they could just go in some morning with a battalion of marines, but there's the matter of those pesky civilian casualties. They're hoping we can clean this up without it becoming any messier than it already is. They've given us two more months."

Buffy blinked. She had not been expecting that last bit of information.

"Then what?" she asked.

Willow shrugged and glanced away sheepishly, a bit of her old self coming out. "I'm guessing napalm."

"What about the people?" Buffy demanded.

"Yeah," Willow agreed. "Time is running short now. We're going to have to go in sooner rather than later. If you learned anything while you were in enemy territory that could help us, well, that's why we hoped you'd be willing to answer some questions."

"Anything," Buffy told her.

The questions began. From Willow. From Ms. Haversham. From Wesley. From Lonergan. Buffy told them everything she could remember about her captivity and escape, and ignored the stares she received when she revealed the circumstances of August's death. She told them about her journey to Sunnydale, her conversation with Parker, the deaths of Harmony and Drusilla, and everything leading up to the moment when they arrived to help her at the border.

Somewhere in the midst of all of that, Wesley asked her where she had gotten the crossbow.

*The crossbow.* Buffy hesitated, glancing uncomfortably around the room.

"On the way into Sunnydale I stopped at the old drive-in there, thinking there might be something I could use for a weapon. I broke up a chair for some stakes. In the projection room, upstairs in the concrete building there, someone had left me a crossbow."

"You mean someone had left a crossbow behind," Wesley corrected, running his fingers through his beard.

"No," Buffy said firmly. "Someone had left it for me. There was a note. 'For Buffy.' "

Everyone in the room stared at her.

Willow broke the silence. "Was it signed?"

Buffy shook her head and then the debate began as to who might have been the one to leave the weapon there, who could have known Buffy would even stop there. It soon became clear that no one could have known such a thing.

"Whoever it was must have been there with you, or right before you. Close enough to've seen you in the parking lot," Lonergan reasoned.

"It was the middle of the day and I didn't see much cover," Buffy noted.

"You never know," Willow told her. "You've seen their sunsuits for yourself. Not high fashion, but they can move around during the day if they're motivated enough."

"But why would anyone do that?" Buffy asked. "Someone was watching me, no question about that. But if it was a vampire, why would they try to help me?"

Willow stared at the table, brows knitted in contemplation. No one else would meet Buffy's gaze. All of them seemed stumped. A low rumble of muttered conversation filled the room. Then Buffy glanced at Wesley, and he was the only one not looking away.

"What if it's Angel?" he asked.

Several people began to talk at once, some to argue the question as ridiculous, others to support the possibility. Buffy's mind was awhirl as she considered it. *Could Angel be alive?*

Before she could respond, however, Lonergan swore

loudly and shot to his feet, one hand clamped to his forehead. He bumped into Ms. Haversham's chair and nearly knocked her over.

His nose had begun to bleed.

"What?" Willow demanded. "Christopher, what is it?"

Lonergan wiped the blood from his upper lip, his expression grave.

"We've got a vampire on the premises."

# Chapter 3

*Bloody hell!*

The bedspread was on fire. It was a delicate pastel floral pattern with black scorch marks, flames licking up from those charred spots. *Of all the soddin' indignities I've had dumped on my head today,* Spike thought. *Hell, of all the drawbacks to being a vampire in general, running about draped in flowery linens is the worst.*

The burning didn't send him into giggling fits, either.

Spike whipped the spread off him and tossed it to the floor, then stamped furiously, almost petulantly on it to put the flames out. Gingerly, he felt his face and found that his eyelashes and eyebrows were little more than tightly curled ashes now. His skin was stiff and cracked and it felt as though if he moved too quickly it might split right open. He did not even want to touch his hair.

He seethed with thoughts of vengeance. Nobody

treated him like this, tossed him out some window to torch in the sun like so much garbage. The loss of Drusilla had left a void inside him, a cold, rotting place where despair and bitterness festered. But that void was not really empty anymore. Hate and rage had seeped into that place and now it was boiling over.

Giles had vision. He had a dream. Spike usually ignored the big-talking vampires; silly gits usually had lots of swagger but little sense. Any tosser could wax poetic about a world crushed beneath the heel of vampire rule, human cattle, an endless feast of babies and virgins. Just a whiff of that sort of bluster usually sent Spike packing, chuckling all the way.

But Giles, now. Rupert Giles had had a plan. Spike had plenty of plans of his own, mind, and the Big Bad was not about to sign on to play lapdog—or even foxhound—to a vampire fresh out of the dirt. Thing was, this was Giles, and Spike and Drusilla had both believed he could pull off this grand scheme.

And what a world that would have been.

Now, though . . . now Spike was pissed. And his day was just getting worse and worse. Flowery linens just one example of the way the world had suddenly turned against him. How he was supposed to look fierce hiding his precious mug from the sun under embroidered carnations and lilies . . . *well, you just can't, is all.*

When Giles had thrown him out the window he had been burned badly. But even with the spread covering him, the time he had spent outside before breaking into the Council installation had been worse, trying to be all sneaky in a decorative spread that also happened to be *on fire.*

Now, to top it all off, he had a sudden craving for a cigarette that he found cruelly ironic, but he had dropped his cigs somewhere along the way.

*Giles,* he thought. *Bloody bastard.*

In his left hand he held the key card he had taken from a guard on the grounds outside. He was tempted to toss it away but then reconsidered. It had gotten him into the building, and there was no way to tell if it would come in handy later. Spike slipped the plastic rectangle into his pocket as he surveyed his surroundings.

A wide corridor, rear of the facility. The building seemed sterile and utilitarian, almost like a hospital. Once upon a time that might have been exactly what it was. *Could do with a visit to the burn center right about now,* he thought, with a smile that cracked his scorched skin and made him curse through gritted teeth.

There were several doors with square glass windows in them along this corridor. He glanced into each room as he moved farther into the building and found mostly abandoned offices and several that seemed like they were still in use. He passed one room in which dozens of white boxes had been stacked floor to ceiling, but did not stop to see what was being stored. To his left, a stairwell led up. Spike figured he was less likely to run into sentries upstairs, and that was probably where he would find personnel quarters.

The Slayer's quarters.

With every step, he winced at the pain in his slowly

healing skin. By the time he reached the top, he was practically snarling. His desire for a cigarette had grown almost obsessive. He knew it was probably just his mind trying to think about anything except pain, but the pain was good in its way. It gave him something to focus on so he wouldn't think about the humiliation.

Spike could take the pain just as well as he could hand it out. There had been plenty of times when pain had been a recreational sport for him and Dru. Pain was a friend, old and dear. Every time he winced and ground his teeth in agony, he could think about other times when he had been the *giver.* Those were sweet memories.

So Spike could take the pain.

The humiliation, on the other hand . . . well, nobody made Spike look like a weakling and lived to boast of it.

There were windows along the second floor corridor and so he hugged the walls to stay out of the sunlight. What he needed now was to find someone to torture information out of. *Shouldn't be too difficult,* he thought. The place stank of humans.

As though he had summoned them by the strength of his will alone, he heard voices beyond a pair of doors ahead that led into another part of the facility. For just a moment, Spike grinned, but it hurt too much.

He threw open the doors.

On the other side was a broad, diamond-shaped atrium where four corridors came together. Several stories up was an enormous, many-paned skylight that spilled sunlight all the way down to the first floor. A balustrade ran all around the atrium, except straight in front of him, where stairs led up from the ground floor.

The atrium was full. Perhaps two dozen Council operatives waited there in the sunshine. Guns cocked. Crossbows were aimed. Several flamethrowers puffed to life. But the worst were the small clutch of people standing just at the top of the stairs, directly across from Spike.

The witch, Willow Rosenberg. A grim-faced Xander Harris, who had proven to be almost supernaturally lucky, practically unkillable. That Watcher, Wesley, who had once run with Angel. A petite little Asian girl he guessed was the latest Slayer. And, of course, the real Slayer. Buffy Summers.

"Hail, hail," Spike said dryly. "The gang's all here. Warms the cockles, it really does."

Then there was Christopher Lonergan, who had a bit of blood just under his nose.

Spike ran a hand over his burned, ragged hair. "Hello, Chris. Didn't know you were in the country."

"Guess you didn't," Lonergan replied. "Else you wouldn'a tried sneaking about in here."

Spike grinned. "Got an extra ciggie?"

The witch took a step toward him. The sunlight gleamed off her red hair and Spike shifted uncomfortably just looking at it. He stood in the shadow of the corridor now, but if they dragged him into the atrium . . . well, he'd had enough sun for one day.

"What are you doing here, Spike? A long way to come just to commit suicide," Willow said curtly.

"Is that what I've done?" Spike asked.

Xander nodded. "Oh, yeah."

"Maybe so," he allowed. Then he tilted his head and shrugged, as though none of it mattered to him in the least. "Gotta say, though, I think you've got bigger fish to slay. You're about twenty steps behind Giles by now, kids. The old sod's got his people in place all over the state. Only a matter of days now before he's got Los Angeles. Blink and you'll miss it."

"Why tell us?" Willow asked.

Spike narrowed his eyes, blistered skin cracking, and studied Buffy. Thus far she had not said a word, but she glared at him with such ferocity that he began to wonder if it had not been a mistake after all, his coming here.

He shrugged. "Bugger pissed me off. He's got big plans, he has, but they don't involve me. I'm off now to redder pastures, but before I left I thought I'd see to it that you did my dirty work for me. In all our best interests, of course."

No one spoke. No one moved. The operatives barely seemed to be breathing. The young Slayer looked a bit nervous, and Spike gave her a friendly smile. The hate-filled sneer he received in return chilled him. But not nearly as much as the expression on Buffy's face.

"Right then," he said with a shrug. "My mistake. You all might want to take a last trip to Disney before the Mouse sprouts fangs." He raised a hand in a small wave. "Ta."

As Spike began to turn, Xander broke ranks and sprinted across the atrium to the double doors. Willow shouted something after him, but nobody else moved. Spike only smiled as he lashed out at Xander.

But he was still healing. His flesh was tight, burned, and those injuries sapped his speed and strength. Xander gripped his throat, drove his head back against the post between the double doors. Spike struck him once, hard, but Xander only grunted and cracked the vampire's head against the post again. Groggy, Spike tried to pull the enraged man's hand away.

Xander struck him in the face, shattering his nose and splitting the burned skin on his cheek. Another blow fell, and another, and all the strength ran out of Spike. When his eyes fluttered open, trying to focus, he saw the stake in Xander's hand.

"This is for Anya, you son of a—"

The stake fell.

Buffy was there. She grabbed Xander's wrist, stopped the point from puncturing Spike's chest, his heart.

Xander spun toward her, practically spitting with rage. "What the hell are you doing?"

Buffy's eyes were dark with painful knowledge. Spike was fascinated by the girl now. He had not gotten a good look at her in the dark the night before, nor on the street during their previous skirmish. In fact, this was the first decent look he'd had at her in years. Her face had thinned slightly, and it made her look meaner. Or maybe that was just her eyes.

"You want to win this?" Buffy told Xander. "We need the information he has."

"Thattagirl," Spike cooed, there on the floor. He sat

up, grimacing with pain. "Knew I could count on you to see the sense of it. Not the first time we've done business, after all. Better the devil you know, yeah?"

In a move so swift Spike barely saw it, Buffy spun and shot out a hard side kick that cracked his cheekbone and slammed him back on the floor. Groaning, Spike tried to rise, tried to scuttle away from her, but the Slayer swept in and kicked him in the side, splintering several ribs.

Enraged and confused, the vampire reached out to her and Buffy snapped his wrist. Then she grabbed him under his chin and, with the prodigious strength of the Chosen One, lifted him off the ground. She carried him back into the atrium and dangled him there, in the sunlight.

Again, Spike began to burn. He screamed in agony this time, for he could feel his skin bubbling, could feel himself start to cook from within, the sun searing the evil in him. It occurred to him, mind reeling from the pain, that there were worse things than flowery linens. That perhaps he was not quite so intimate with pain as he had imagined.

"Bloody hell," he croaked. "Stop!"

Buffy tossed him into the shadow of the double doors where he crumbled into a blackened, whimpering heap.

The Slayer stood over him. "My mother," she said, voice thick with disgust and hate.

Spike grimaced. "Heard about that, did you? Just doing what I was told. Giles gave that order. He was real specific about it."

Ignoring him, she turned to Xander. "We'll find out what he knows. After that, I don't care what you do to him."

Willow stared out her office window at a trio of gulls that circled lazily in the sky. The ocean was thirty miles away and it always made her curious to see the sea birds inland. She wondered if something had drawn them here, or if they had simply become so distracted by their interplay that they had drifted far from their usual haunts. They had a freedom Willow envied.

There was a rap at the door. Willow turned her attention back to her office, which—with its potted plants and the art that hung on the wall—was just about the only room in the entire facility with any warmth. It was her retreat, a place for contemplation, and she rarely liked to have difficult conversations there. But for once she thought that she ought to extend the warmth of this room to another.

"Come in," she called.

The door clicked open and Wesley poked his head in. "We're a bit early, Willow. Sorry about that."

"It's fine," she replied.

He smiled and opened the door all the way to reveal Anna Kuei in the hall behind him. Then Wesley stood aside and ushered the nascent Slayer into the office. There were a pair of black leather chairs in front of Willow's desk, and the two visitors sat and faced her.

"Anna. I'm sorry if this morning's debriefing disturbed you," Willow said kindly.

The girl twirled the fingers of her left hand in the

short tufts of her shocking pink hair. She had the appearance of the rebel, but Willow knew her as a sweet girl, almost an innocent.

"It's all right, Miss Rosenberg," Anna said. Always soft-spoken, her voice today sounded more girlish and wispy than ever.

"Willow, Anna. You're the Slayer now. Call me Willow."

The girl smiled and sat up a bit straighter. "Willow. I just . . ."

When her words trailed off, Wesley jumped in for her. "Anna had a few questions about the, shall we say, dynamics of the Council's efforts here, now that Buffy has returned to the fold."

Willow's brow furrowed. "Shoot."

Anna shrugged, glanced away. "I mean, I know she's the Lost Slayer and everything, and it's like this big deal. But she isn't anything like Faith, is she?"

A tiny smile played upon Willow's lips. During the months of training Anna had spent in this facility with several other Slayers-in-Waiting—girls the Council had pinpointed as having the potential to become the Chosen One—Faith had taken a day to instruct them each time she returned to the facility.

"No," Willow agreed. "She's nothing like Faith."

Anna nodded emphatically. "No kidding. I mean, Faith was all about discipline and focus, and the Lost Slayer—"

"Buffy," Wesley quietly corrected her.

"Buffy," Anna continued. "She's, like, totally unhinged. Okay, nobody's crying over Spike getting his ass handed to him. As long as he ends up dusted, he deserves whatever he gets beforehand. But there's more to it than that. In the debriefing, I just . . . when she talked about August . . ."

The girl's eyes became moist and she wiped a hand across them. Willow's heart went out to her. Anna and August had been close friends during their training, before Faith's death had led to August's being Chosen.

"She killed August," Anna said, hurt and angry. "And now it's supposed to be August's fault, but August isn't here to defend herself."

Wesley reached out and touched Anna's hand to comfort her, but his eyes never left Willow. "She doesn't realize how close you and Buffy are," Wesley said.

"It's all right," Willow said, gaze still on Anna. "I understand what you're feeling. I really do. In high school, Buffy was my best friend. I guess she still is. But it's going to take time for all of us to adjust. There's no way to know what her years in that cell might have done to her. But, for what it's worth, the Buffy Summers I knew would never have killed a human, never mind a Slayer. I believe it was an accident. You know as well as I do, Anna, that August was having problems with the pressure of being Chosen even before she was captured."

"Okay, maybe so," Anna said, her Cupid's-bow lips pinched into a round little pout. "But I hope nobody expects me to be friends with her or something."

"No," Willow said carefully, "but Buffy is a part of the team now. Probably going to be an important part. You could learn a lot from her."

The girl opened her mouth and then clamped it shut tight, and Willow knew she probably had a dozen sarcastic retorts that were bursting to get out.

"The team was fine," Anna said at last. "I mean, if you've got Buffy, what do you need me for? And why does it seem like she's suddenly in charge? Like everyone's looking to her for the next move? You're the one in charge. I don't understand why—"

"Actually, Ms. Haversham is the director of this operation," Willow corrected, feeling a bit awkward.

"Oh, that's crap," Anna snapped. "You're in charge and you know it. Haversham hardly even pretends to be the boss anymore, except in meetings. Even Lonergan looks to you. But Buffy's got this air about her, like everyone should follow her lead."

Wesley scratched at his beard and shifted a bit in his seat. "Her presence does seem to have upset the balance of power somewhat. There's the potential for great confusion there, and in an operation of this magnitude, confusion could be deadly. The mission parameters clearly state that Anna and I are to lead the main unit when the assault on Sunnydale is finally launched. Why do I have the sense that Buffy's arrival is sure to throw a wrench in the works?

"I must confess, Willow, I'm concerned. My experiences with Buffy were limited, of course, and there was always the question of how much of each mission's planning was Buffy's doing and how much was Giles's strategy. Certainly Buffy never allowed *me* to truly lead. My point is that she is rash. The deployment of forces and the creation of layers of strategy for contingencies are hardly her forte. She leads by charisma and passion, by inspiration. Those are enviable traits, to be sure, but leadership also requires forethought, the ability to envision and consider the big picture. Logic, reason, intuition and, frankly, the capacity to outthink your enemy.

"You are far younger than I am, Willow, but I have never questioned your leadership skills. There is a reason why those who were put here to run this operation have tacitly acknowledged you as the de facto commander of this little outpost. You may not give the orders, but you make the decisions.

"It would not only be a travesty to have your leadership jeopardized by Buffy's arrival, formidable warrior though she is, but in my humble opinion it could also have a catastrophic impact on our chances of success."

Wesley paused for a moment, then nodded his head once, brusquely, as if physically punctuating his thoughts on the matter. Then he took a deep breath and let it out slowly as he sat back in his chair.

Willow placed her elbows on her desk and leaned forward, fingers steepled under her chin. She studied the two of them closely. Anna's emotional response to Buffy's revelations—even her mere presence—was understandable and genuine. Wesley, on the other hand . . .

"Are you concerned about Buffy stealing *my* thunder, or your own, as the current Watcher?" Willow asked him.

Wesley sputtered a bit, muttered something about the question being preposterous, but he would not meet her gaze. He had always been easy for her to read.

"You were *her* Watcher briefly, Wes, or don't you remember?" Willow prodded, her gaze roving from him to Anna and back again. "I don't know how the years she's been gone have affected Buffy. Goddess knows I hope my friend is still there. I'm going to try to find out."

Willow hesitated for a moment, unsure whether or not to confide in them. Of late, there seemed no one she felt comfortable confiding in. When she had first seen Buffy again she had been so thrilled that she had let all the intervening years drop away as if they had never been, but it had not taken long for her to put walls up around her heart again. She wanted her best friend back so very much, but she would not allow that desire to override her common sense. She had responsibilities that were greater than her own needs.

At last, she decided that revealing her own fears to these two would be harmless enough. Willow glanced at Wesley, but then regarded Anna more closely.

"I knew Giles very well before," she said. "Wesley did, too, but he likes to pretend Giles wasn't as cunning as we both know he is. I have a confession to make. I've believed for a very long while that it was only a matter of time before all this blew up on us, and the U.S. government would have to essentially declare war on southern California. If Spike's telling the truth about L.A.—hello! A little more right than I ever wanted to be."

The young Slayer's eyes sparkled with fear. She shook her head in denial. Wesley cleared his throat, but did not argue.

"The thing is, if Buffy's really back, I mean, y'know, if she hasn't slipped a gear after all that time to herself, she may be our best chance at stopping this before we reach the point of no return. I don't know about Buffy now, but Buffy *then,* my friend? If anyone can stop Giles, she could."

They stared at her.

Willow smiled. "If that means the balance of power is going to shift? Not exactly going to argue."

As soon as Xander hauled open the steel door, Buffy caught the scent of burned flesh from within the room. Her stomach convulsed and her nostrils flared with disgust. From that point on, she breathed through her mouth.

At dusk, Willow and Xander had come to fetch her from her quarters and then escorted her down to dinner. Things were awkward. Though she wished for the closeness and humor they had once shared, it was almost all business. After they had eaten, Xander had led the way down into the basement and to a wing to the rear of the building that had been transformed into holding cells.

There was one door that had several dents in it and Buffy could hear something huge grunting and shambling within. She glanced at Willow, but her friend had not even seemed to hear it. Buffy decided not to bother asking.

Now, though, they had arrived at the cell where Spike had been imprisoned since early that day.

When Xander pulled the door open the rest of the way and flicked on the lights, Spike was crouched in a defensive posture in a far corner of the room. The extensive burns that had covered his body earlier were not gone, but they had improved significantly. His hair had even begun to grow back somewhat. There were places on his skin where the flesh was raw and wet, pink and vulnerable. Healing.

Spike's face changed instantly, his brow thickening, fangs lengthening. He snarled, low and dangerous, as Xander approached.

"You had me at a bit of a disadvantage before, boy," Spike said, voice a rasp. "I'm feelin' better now. You shouldn't have left me alone all this time."

Xander grinned, and the expression was so haunting that Buffy shivered. Then he pulled a simple plastic water pistol from the small of his back as though it were a real gun. He leveled it at Spike and fired several hissing squirts of holy water into the vampire's face.

Spike's flesh bubbled and steamed as though the water were acid, eating into his skin. With an agonizing scream, the vampire covered his eyes. Xander clasped his hands together and brought them around in a single, massive blow to the side of Spike's head. Spike went down, clutching his ribs where Buffy had kicked him earlier. Xander crouched in front of him and aimed the water pistol at his face again.

"I never liked it when you called me 'boy,' even when I was one," he said pleasantly. "You want to know why we let you heal? It's 'cause you were so far gone that we didn't think torture would be effective. You're living in the past, Spike. Not so much your glory days anymore, as your final hour."

Spike managed to lift his chin but his defiant expression did not reach his eyes, which were filled with fear. The room suddenly seemed too small, too close. The atmosphere had turned ominous, even cruel. This wild thing they had trapped was a vicious, savage beast, but there was nothing honorable about these proceedings now.

They were in a killing box.

"You used to be funny, you know that?" Spike sneered at Xander. "Not very, and stupid humor, yeah, but at least you had a soddin' *sense* of humor. That water gun gag? That wasn't funny."

"I haven't felt funny in a long time." Xander squirted holy water into Spike's hair and the vampire swore and started slapping at his head to stop the burning. Xander chuckled softly. "Now that, though? That's funny."

The twin souls that existed within Buffy were in conflict as she watched. The older Buffy, who had truly experienced the years of imprisonment and torment, the electrical prods and beatings, the knowledge of her own defeat, had not a moment's hesitation about Xander's treatment of Spike. But Buffy-at-nineteen felt differently. To her, only weeks had passed since a simpler time. It seemed almost perverse now to look back upon that chaos and realize that it was, indeed, simpler. Better. Brighter.

"If this is bothering you, you can step out," Willow suggested quietly.

Buffy flinched and turned to stare at her. It occurred to her that as Willow developed her magick more, she might well have found herself able to read thoughts, or at least sense emotions.

"I'm fine," Buffy replied, somewhat defensive.

"You seem pretty conflicted." Willow gazed at her with obvious concern.

"It's . . . it's not this. We'll talk later," Buffy promised.

"All right."

"You done?" Xander snapped. "Can we get on with it?"

Buffy narrowed her gaze. "Why don't we? In fact, why don't we just get right to it."

"Do your worst," Spike grunted. "I woulda just told you everything you'd like to know and got the hell out of town. But now? You get nothing."

Willow shook her head and *tsk*ed like the teacher she briefly was, once upon a time. "You don't really think we could let you go?"

"Did once," Spike replied with a sniff of hauteur. He looked at Buffy. "Me and the Slayer had a deal back then, didn't we, Buffy? Weren't too good for old Spike in those days."

"I had to choose between killing you and averting the

Apocalypse, Spike," Buffy said. "It was a harder decision than you'll ever know, but I figured I'd always get another shot at you."

"And here we are," Willow said, but without humor.

Buffy was relieved to see that, unlike Xander, she did not seem to get any pleasure out of this situation.

Slowly, defiantly, Spike struggled to stand. "To hell with the lot of you," the vampire said. "Do it."

Xander raised the water pistol again, but Buffy had had enough. She reached into the deep pocket of her oversize sweatshirt and pulled out a stake Willow had given her, then shoved past Xander and grabbed Spike by the throat for the second time that day.

He did not even bother to defend himself. "What are you gonna do, Slayer?"

Buffy slammed him against the wall, held him there, and drove the long stake right through the center of his chest, splitting ribs. Spike roared with the pain of it, but his eyes were wide with surprise as well, for Buffy had purposely avoided his heart.

The stake jutted out four inches. With an open palm, Buffy slammed it home, drove it deeper into his body until it was buried all the way. Spike growled and tried to move, and only then did he realize that the stake really had gone *all* the way through.

Buffy had pinned him to the wall.

She put her face up, only an inch from his. "Remember me mentioning how you killed my mother?"

Spike sagged a bit, hung there on the stake.

"Xander isn't pretending, Spike. Neither is Willow.

Things have changed. You better wake up to that right now," Buffy told him. Then she glanced over at the others. "Hurt him. Do whatever you have to do to get the information we need and do *not* let him die until we have it."

Buffy turned away from him, crossed the room and leaned there, opposite Spike, her arms crossed.

Xander and Willow started toward him, and Spike's bravado collapsed. "All right," he said. "All right!"

For hours they asked questions about Giles's operations in Sunnydale and beyond, and Spike answered. The Council had spies there, of course, mostly humans posing as vampire worshipers. They had been able to provide a great deal of information about the various nests and lairs that Giles's minions had established in Sunnydale, and Spike confirmed all of that information. A great deal of what he told them, the Council already knew. But he also revealed that Giles had already turned a sizable percentage of the LAPD, a number of Hollywood executives, and the mayor of Los Angeles. With that kind of infiltration already in place, L.A. might well be under tacit vampire rule within months, or even weeks. And that was only the beginning.

A shiver went through Buffy. Giles had the wisdom and the patience to fulfill his ambitions. Unless someone stopped him, he would slowly, inexorably, take over the state of California and then spread his influence from there.

Buffy knew that the federal government had secretly

told the Council they would resort to full-scale military assault if necessary. The civilian casualties would be enormous and there was no guarantee that Giles himself would be destroyed. Even worse than that, however, was Buffy's fear that the government would not act quickly enough, that they would be so afraid of public backlash at massive destruction on American soil that they might hesitate to act.

If Spike's information was right, if he were telling the truth, the Council had to act quickly. Any other resolution to the situation would be disastrous.

It was after ten o'clock at night when they were through with Spike. He was still pinned to the wall. Buffy stretched, stiff from standing in one place for so long. When she glanced over at her old friends, she found them both watching her expectantly, particularly Xander.

Buffy nodded grimly.

Xander did not smile. Instead he reached for a stake he kept in a sheath clipped to his belt at the small of his back. He brought it out and Spike grimaced when he saw it, as though even now he did not really believe it was over.

Buffy expected to feel something, some emotional conflict or simply melancholy. But for all his charisma, all the times it had seemed he might be an ally, Spike was a vampire. He had slaughtered Buffy's mother, and Anya, and hundreds, probably thousands of others.

There was only one way the night could end.

"This is for Anya," Xander said.

He staked Spike through the heart. The vampire's eyes went wide and he snarled at Xander.

"Oh, you rotten bast—" he said.

Then he exploded in a puff of cinder and ash.

They agreed to return to their rooms to wash up, and then reconvene in the conference room in half an hour, just the three of them.

But when Buffy got back to her quarters, Giles was waiting.

# CHAPTER 4

A ripple of disquiet went through Buffy as she pushed open the door to her room. It was dark within, and the feeling that some peril lurked there was instant and certain. Buffy stepped inside and reached for the light switch, but she hesitated. Something moved in the dark, then, a figure unfolding from the shadows, silhouetted only by the starlight from outside the window.

The window where there was no longer any screen.

"Shut the door," whispered the figure in a voice so familiar that Buffy forgot to breathe.

Her hand fell away from the light switch and her eyes began to adjust to the dark. "Why would I want to do that?"

"So we can talk. I think it's time, don't you? Time we talk?"

Despite the glare of the lights from the hall, she could see enough now to know that it really was him. Rupert

Giles made no attempt to remain in the shadows. He slipped away from the wall and leaned, instead, on the sill of the open window. There was still a smattering of gray in his brown hair. He wore tan pants and a rust-colored V-neck sweater pushed up at the sleeves. In short, he looked for all the world like the man she had abandoned to Camazotz years before, save for one detail.

He no longer wore glasses.

Guilt cut Buffy deeply, for she had blamed herself from the moment Willow had told her Giles was a vampire. Though she had been following every lesson he had ever taught her by doing so, she had left Giles behind five years ago. This was the result.

Not just the monster he had become, but the nightmare he had made of what had once been her world.

"Oh, come now, Buffy," Giles said, his tone as impatient as she remembered. "Far be it for me to tell you not to feel badly, but at least try to focus, please? Now, why don't you close the door so we can have a civil conversation without being interrupted."

Buffy's throat was dry. She swallowed, stood up a bit straighter. *It isn't Giles anymore,* she reminded herself. *This is not him, not any more than Angelus was Angel. It's just a parasite, a thing living inside his remains, making it walk and talk, like a marionette.*

She had to remember that. In some ways, she knew, the vampire even *thought* it was Giles. It had his memories, his personality traits, but it was not him.

"All right," she said, blinking as though waking from a dream. "Let's talk."

Buffy stepped aside and closed the door, casting the room into deeper darkness for a moment. The eyes of the vampire flickered orange in that darkness, cruel pinpoints like poisoned stars in the night sky.

Then she turned on the light.

Giles smiled sheepishly. "Well, that's better, isn't it? Does take away some of the mystery though, doesn't it?"

Buffy snaked a hand into the deep front pocket of her oversize sweatshirt and withdrew the stake. Her fingers flexed around it, testing its weight.

"Tell me why I shouldn't just kill you right now? All our problems would be over."

Giles had been studying her, a smirk on his features. Now his gaze seemed to linger on her for a moment too long before he blinked and a quizzical expression came over his face.

"Hmm?" he asked.

A chill deep as the marrow swept through her then. *It's not him,* she insisted to herself. But that hesitation, that moment lost in thought, was such a part of who Giles was that it unnerved her even more. She considered the possibility that it might have been a bit of show for her benefit, but it had seemed so real, so unconscious. Ever since the world of vampires had been revealed to her she had believed that the creatures were just spiritual squatters, taking up residence in empty husks. She had needed to believe that in order to fulfill her duties, to dust vampires without hesitation.

But this thing . . . that single moment made her realize that in all the ways that mattered, all the ways that would hurt her, it *was* Giles. Not the man she had known, not her Watcher, but somehow Giles nevertheless.

Buffy felt as though she were being torn apart.

As though he knew precisely what she was feeling, Giles's expression softened. Again, it was a look she was so familiar with, as though he wanted to reach out to her but was troubled by the emotions at hand, not at all adept at offering comfort.

The look was a lie. A mockery of all that Giles had once meant to her. It shook her free of her pain. Her fingers gripped the stake and she launched herself across the room at him.

His evasion was so swift that he seemed to slip between moments. Buffy struck out with her left fist, then her right, she whirled into a kick that had so much force it ought to have decapitated him.

Not a single blow struck him.

Giles did not smile now, did not mock or taunt her.

But he hit her, a backhand that sent her pirouetting down to the floor. Sweeping around like a scythe blade, she tried to knock his legs out from under him, but he danced lightly away.

Again, she pressed the attack. Once, twice, her blows missed. But now she had extracted herself from the moment, examining the conflict as though it were a chess match. Her attack now was merely a feint to draw another punch from Giles.

When he struck out at her a second time, she was ready. Buffy sidestepped, grabbed his left wrist and then twirled into his arms as though they were engaged in a macabre waltz. The stake held tightly to her, she wrapped herself in his left arm and then thrust the stake at his chest.

Giles stopped the wooden point with his right hand; it pierced the palm and then the tip appeared at the back of his hand, protruding from the skin. Buffy withdrew the stake and stabbed it down again, but the wraithlike vampire slipped away from her.

"Well done, Buffy," he said. "Bravo, truly. I couldn't be more proud. It makes me realize that coming here was precisely the right thing to do."

Wary, Buffy stood ready for another skirmish. Giles gestured toward the bed.

"I brought you a gift."

Even as she glanced over toward the bed, the vampire crossed the room and lifted a sword from the mattress. Its hilt was steel and wood and leather, not at all ornate and yet somehow elegant. The scabbard was black and plain, but when Giles drew the sword out, Buffy saw that the blade was inscribed with runes all along its length.

Giles turned the sword in his hand and starlight glimmered off the blade.

"For you," he whispered.

"I don't want anything from you," she snapped.

"But I insist."

"Fine, give it to me. Just the thing I need to cut your head off."

He smirked. "What else would you say?"

Suddenly there was no trace of the old Giles in his

features, in his stance. It was as though the evil that burrowed inside him had emerged for a moment to gaze upon her with its own eyes.

The air seemed charged with the power that crackled within him, his eyes flickering with jack-o'-lantern flame.

"You might be able to kill me, Buffy," he confessed, though without losing his haughty air. "But it won't be easy. You think it's only speed that saved me tonight? You're nearly as fast as I am, maybe faster. But I trained you, remember? I'm inside your mind, crawling inside your skin. I'm the only real father you ever had, the only one who cared about you. I know every move you'll make before it's even been born in that ferocious brain of yours.

"Still, you might be able to kill me. If you really want to."

Suddenly it was too warm in the room. What little air rustled the curtains was stagnant and damp. Buffy felt her breath hitching in her chest; a vein pulsed in her temple; her heart beat too loud inside her head.

Hate and despair filled her in equal portions, but were inextricably tangled.

"What makes you think I won't?" she whispered.

Giles smiled, cocked his head to one side like a wolf listening for the steps of its prey.

"Hope," he said. "I forged you just as that sword was forged, Buffy. You belong at my side just as it should hang at yours. I was curious how you would change after so long without human contact. When you finally escaped, I observed you closely. I aided you as best I could. I had to see with my own eyes that the weapon I had forged had retained its fine edge. And you have, my dear. Truly, you have."

Horrible understanding bloomed in Buffy's mind. "The crossbow. You're the one who left it for me."

"Of course," Giles said, seemingly offended. "Wouldn't have been sporting if I hadn't given you a fighting chance. And now you have a choice to make. I am a creature out of time, Buffy. The years have no bearing on me. I can afford to be patient as I spread my influence slowly, quietly, until the world is roughly awakened one night to discover that their lives are no longer their own.

"You should be with me, Buffy. You may not be my daughter, but you *can* be, if only you surrender yourself to fate. Can't you hear the voice of destiny in this?"

Her fingers gripped the stake in her hand. "Oh yeah," she said. "I hear it. It's saying maybe you should start watching the clock again, 'cause your time is up."

Cautiously, her eyes on the sword in his hands, she slipped toward him.

"Ah, well," he said, a mischievous twinkle in his eyes. "Perhaps you require a bit more time to contemplate the future."

With a single fluid motion he cocked his right arm back and hurled the sword at her as though it were a spear. Buffy sidestepped the ancient blade, her left hand whipped out, and she plucked it from the air, then turned to face him with the sword in one hand and the stake in the other.

But Giles was gone.

The curtains billowed as the breeze picked up, but only the stars and the broad lawn behind the installation were visible through the screenless window. Buffy went and leaned on the sill. For a moment she was baffled as to how Giles had made his entry. Her room was much too far above the ground for him to have climbed. Then she glanced up, and understood. Somehow he had reached the roof, come across the top of the place and then hung down to her window from there.

There was no sign of him on the grass below save for the screen he had torn from her window. At least, that was what Buffy thought at first. Then she noticed a dark form a ways from the building, the starlight not enough to make out much detail.

Her gaze fell upon a second. Then, far off to the right, only a few feet from the building's foundation, a third.

Council operatives. Sentries.

Dead men.

The moon was little more than a sliver as the werewolf trailed the scent Giles had left behind. The incongruity of it still astonished Buffy. It was not supposed to happen this way. Yet Oz had strolled casually out onto the lawn with twenty people in tow, found a spot roughly beneath Buffy's window, and sniffed the air.

He had glanced at Willow with eyes heavy with warning. "Keep them back," he had said.

Then he had changed. Buffy had seen him transform under the power of the moon before, but this was different. It looked more painful, and that was saying quite a bit. His body contorted, his facial structure stretched and popped, and as the fur sprouted all over his flesh, Oz arched his back and snarled with the effort of it.

When the transformation was complete, Oz had growled low and dangerous at the people gathered around him. The Council operatives backed off and the werewolf set out on the trail.

Now they followed him as he tracked an invisible trail across the ground. Buffy wrinkled her nose at the werewolf's musky odor and wondered how Oz could smell anything other than himself. When the wolf came to one of the dead sentries, he nudged the corpse a bit, snuffled in its clothes, and then glanced toward a stand of trees on the far side of the property. Oz began to lope toward the small wooded area and then it was just a matter of the rest of them keeping up.

The operatives spread out to run. Buffy found herself in the lead with Willow and Xander to her left and Christopher Lonergan to her right. Wesley and the new Slayer were there as well, but they were back among a group of Council agents who trailed slightly.

Out of the corner of her eye, Buffy saw Willow watching her.

"So, I'm guessing we don't have to invite them in," she said as she ran.

"It was a hospital once. Anyone is welcome in a public place like that. When we first moved in, I tried half a dozen times to cast a spell to revoke that general invitation, but it never took. When a hospital is built, the intention of everyone involved is that it be open to anyone. I think that intent of purpose is too strong to override."

Ahead, Oz had reached the line of trees. The werewolf paused and stared back at them, poised impatiently as they hurried to catch up.

"Meaning any vampire can stroll right in at any time," Buffy said. "Nobody thinks that's a security risk?"

"Of course it is," Lonergan grunted, obviously a bit annoyed. "That's one of the reasons they've got me around here. Bloodsuckers nearby, I sense it."

"So I noticed," Buffy replied. "But you didn't sense Giles, did you?"

Lonergan shot her a withering glance. "Didn't know you'd dusted Spike, did I? Gift I've got can't distinguish one from the other. Just tells me when there's evil about. Look, we've got enough manpower to repel a demon or vampire assault. But, hell, nobody ever thought the leeches'd come in one at a time. Suicide, isn't it?"

"Or it should be," Xander muttered darkly.

Buffy shot him a sidelong glance. "What the hell's that supposed to mean?"

"Nothing."

At the edge of the trees, the Slayer stopped. The other operatives went on around them, but Willow and Xander hung back. The three of them studied one another warily. Buffy could not even bear to argue with Xander. Instead, she looked at Willow.

"So you think, what, that because it's Giles, I let him go?" she demanded.

Willow met her gaze evenly, though she replied with some hesitation. "It crossed my mind."

Xander was more direct. "You can't tell us it wasn't difficult for you, seeing him like that."

"Of course it was!" Buffy snapped, shaking her head. "But that only makes me want to destroy that thing even more. He was too fast for me. That took me by surprise. He trained me, and he used that against me. But if you guys think I just let him go, after all he's done . . . I don't know what you've gone through the last five years that's changed you so much, but you don't know me at all anymore."

Xander stared at her. "Maybe we don't," he said. Then he turned and jogged into the trees after the others.

Buffy watched him go, then stared at Willow. A bitter sort of anger rose up in her and she turned to follow Xander. After a few steps, though, she changed her mind, turned and confronted Willow.

"When they put me in that cell, they didn't just take away my freedom. They stole so much more from me. My mother. Giles. Faith. Angel. And five years of my life. I guess I didn't realize they'd stolen you from me, too."

Willow blanched, all the wary hesitation going out of her expression in an instant. She took a quick, unsteady breath and shook her head almost imperceptibly. Buffy waited for a few seconds for her to speak, but when Willow said nothing, she turned to follow Xander through the trees. The woods weren't very deep, perhaps thirty feet. On the other side was an office park. The werewolf was crouched on a spot in the parking lot, sniffing the pavement. He glanced up expectantly. In that form Oz could not speak, but his meaning was clear.

This was where the trail stopped.

Buffy hung back, watching Xander and Lonergan and the other operatives begin to scan the lot for any sign of Giles, but it was clear they all knew it was a futile pursuit.

There was a rustle from the woods behind her, and then Willow laid a hand on Buffy's shoulder. The Slayer turned to face her old friend, and was surprised to see that Willow seemed almost angry.

"There's something you should understand," Willow said. For a moment, she glanced away, then fixed her gaze upon Buffy again. "After they took you, it was a while before we realized what was really going on. Giles took his time, covered his tracks. During that time before it all really went to hell, there wasn't a day that went by that I didn't think the next phone call, the next knock on the door, was going to be you. That you'd find a way to get free, to come back. That you'd have a plan.

"When Angel went looking for you and he didn't come back either . . . I still tried to tell myself it would be all right. We searched for you constantly, interrogated every vamp and demon in Sunnydale. I tried to use magick to find you, but I knew that was probably useless. Giles would have expected that."

Willow pressed her lips together and turned away, wiping at her eyes.

"A little more than a year after they took you, the vampires rose up and took Sunnydale. It happened in a single night, and we had no idea there were so many of them. A lot of the cops. The mayor. People's parents. *My* parents, Buffy."

With a small shudder, Buffy put a hand over her mouth. "Oh God, Willow."

"I hadn't been by the house for a couple of weeks," Willow went on, eyes narrowing with grief at the memory. "That night, they came to see me."

"What . . . what did you do?"

Willow shook her head and glanced off at some point in the distance, as though she could still see the horrors she had witnessed that day.

"Not me," she said softly, the burden of her memories clear in the set of her shoulders, the cast of her eyes. "Oz. He dusted them both. It's never been the same with us since then. I never stopped hoping you would be all right. But after that night, I couldn't wait for you anymore, you know?"

Regret weighed heavily upon Buffy and she cursed herself for being so selfish. She was not the only one whose world had changed.

"I'm sorry I wasn't there for you," Buffy said. "But, Willow, I'm here *now.*"

A tiny, hopeful smile twitched upon Willow's lips. Her hand shook a bit as she held it out. Buffy took it, their fingers twining together. Then the two women embraced briefly.

"I'm so glad you're alive," Willow whispered.

"Join the club," Buffy replied as they separated again. "So what's our next move?"

"You're asking me?"

"Seems like you're the girl to ask around here."

Willow furrowed her brow in contemplation. "If even half of what Spike said about Giles's advancements in Los Angeles were true, and after this thing with Giles, I think we have to accelerate our plans. But I want to talk to Christopher and Ms. Haversham first."

Buffy nodded slowly, then paused. "Before you do that, though? There are some other things we should talk about."

Willow stared at Buffy, astonished and baffled. "Is that even possible?"

Buffy threw up her hands, a kind of lost expression on her face. "Apparently."

They sat on the sofa in Willow's quarters, shoes off, feet drawn up beneath them as they faced each other. After they had come back inside, Willow had brought Buffy here. The Slayer had been distracted as she complimented Willow on how nice the suite was, the way Willow had acquired some of the things that decorated the walls and shelves. Though Willow had known Buffy was stalling, putting off getting around to discussing whatever was on her mind, she could never have prepared herself for the sheer incredulity of it.

"Are you sure it isn't . . . well, no offense, but some

kind of psychosis from being a prisoner so long?" she ventured.

Buffy shook her head. "It would be easier if I was crazy, huh? Tell me about it. But, not, sorry to say."

Willow rested her chin atop her knees, arms wrapped tightly around her shins, and stared at Buffy as she turned the extraordinary story over and over in her mind.

"Tell me that look is from you puzzling out how to fix it," Buffy said hopefully.

"Sort of that," Willow replied hesitantly. "And sort of . . . there are really two of you in there?"

"Yep. *Dos* Buffys."

"There's no conflict, though? No struggle for dominance or whatever?"

Buffy gave her a sheepish look. "Haven't thought about it much, to be honest. Been a little busy. But it isn't like having two different minds in one body. Two sets of memories, yeah, but not really. I mean, the stuff that happened five years ago . . . all that's a lot fresher in my mind than it should be, because in a crazy way it just happened a few *weeks* ago. I know there's this doubled up thing happening, but both of the souls in me *are* me. Y'know?"

"If I say I do, will you not try to explain it anymore? It's making my head hurt."

"I know how you feel," Buffy said. "I mean, some of the things that I do, I'm not even sure if my instincts and emotions come from version nineteen-point-oh or twenty-four-point-oh, or some combination of both. But it's not like I'm all Jekyll and Hyde or anything."

Willow nodded, but her mind was already skipping tracks, examining other aspects of this bizarre phenomenon. "Let me think out loud for a second." She stood up and paced around the room a bit, reaching out to touch familiar, comforting objects, thoughts swirling. At the same time, even though she was contemplating Buffy's situation, in the back of her mind a warm, joyful feeling had begun to grow now that the awkwardness she had felt toward Buffy had been dispersed.

"This is thinking out loud?" Buffy asked.

"Oh, sorry," Willow replied quickly, waving at something in the air around her. "It's just . . . a little overwhelming. It's hard to put any of it into words."

Buffy leaned forward on the sofa. "Those telepathic powers I had once? Long gone."

"I know, I know. All right, since your *now* self remembers being thrown into the cell in the first place, and since I'm pretty sure you were *you* for a second there after Camazotz ripped Zotzilaha out of you, we know this, um, overcrowding thing is temporary. Which means we're destined to figure out how to send you back."

With a sigh, Willow reached up and took the clip from her hair, then shook it out. Her head hurt, and though she doubted the clip was responsible, it felt better to have her hair down.

"That's not right, is it?" she asked.

Buffy shook her head. "I wish it was that simple. But

no, that's not right. Even if you can figure out how to separate me, or us, or whatever, and send me back to where I belong, if you just put me in at that moment, nothing will have changed. Everything will happen the same way."

Willow nodded. "Which means that Camazotz exorcising The Prophet from your *then-body* is the catalyst, the thing that draws you back from this time." Alarm bells went off inside her. "And we have no way of knowing when that will happen. It could be years or seconds from now."

"Exactly," Buffy said. "The clock is ticking but we don't know how much time we have. Before I get pulled back, you've got to figure out how to override it all and send me back farther, back *before* The Prophet Zotzilla or whatever took over my body. Zotzilaha said I made a mistake that led to this. I hate to say it, but I believe that. Which means I have to go back and stop myself from making that mistake; I have to pick the right moment."

Willow pressed a hand to her forehead. "Which is?"

Buffy sighed. "I don't know. I guess I made a lot of mistakes. The thing that sticks out in my mind was that night at the harbor master's office, when Giles was captured. I . . . left him behind."

"You had to," Willow told her. "You'd probably both have been killed right then and there. What could you have done differently?"

The Slayer lowered her gaze and a shadow fell across her face. "I don't know. Maybe it wasn't that moment.

Maybe the specific moment was before that. Or even after it. But what could I have done differently? I want you to use your magick to give me a chance to find out. I'll tell you this much, though. If I get a second chance, I'll never leave Giles behind again."

"I wish I had as much faith in me as you do," Willow said with a soft laugh. "But Zotzilaha did this to you. Once we understand exactly what she did and we can figure out how she did it, hopefully we'll be able to reverse it. If we can get you back far enough, none of this will ever have happened. Everything in my life will be different."

Buffy frowned. "Will, I'm sorry, I didn't even think about that. But—"

Willow interrupted firmly. "Anything's better than this." All the heartaches of the past five years came to her then with crystal clarity. The death and loss and disappointment, and the loneliness.

"I'm so glad you're here," she said.

Buffy gave her an emphatic nod and a sweet smile. "Never thought I'd say this, but me too."

"I'm going to get on the research right away," Willow promised.

"Good. While we're waiting around for that, we can work on the plan."

"Plan?"

"How to take Sunnydale back and kill Giles."

"Ah," Willow nodded. "That plan."

Over the years since Sunnydale had fallen to the vampires, its downtown area had become like Bourbon

Street in New Orleans. While some shops and restaurants still had windows boarded up, there was more life here than anywhere else in town.

After dark, at least.

The old Sun Cinema was technically closed, its façade falling apart, but they still showed movies all night, every night, thanks to one enterprising demon who saw a need and filled it. Establishments that had been trashed or abandoned had been replaced over time with others, mostly bars and strip clubs and such.

Giles rode north through town on a refurbished thirty-year-old Norton motorcycle that was his pride and joy. He had first spotted the machine in Aaron Trask's garage eighteen months earlier. Trask was the human mechanic who cared for all the vehicles used by Giles and his most trusted aides. For more than a year, in his spare time, Giles had admired the mechanic's handiwork as he restored the Norton. When it was finished, buffed to a high shine, ready to go, Giles let Trask take it out for one ride before he demanded the motorcycle as tribute to the king.

Frankly he thought the whole king thing was a load of crap, but he found that vampires and humans were, as a general rule, stupid, and royalty was something they could understand. That, and fear. Giles had a feeling it was more the latter than the former that convinced Aaron Trask to hand over the Norton without a word of argument.

Trask hated him, that much was clear to Giles. For that alone, he would have killed the man, but he was a very good mechanic.

A short time later Giles parked the motorcycle in its

spot in the garage under City Hall. The guards all inclined their heads as he passed. Aaron Trask was there working on a limousine as Giles walked to the elevator bank, past a pair of sentries on duty there. He smiled and waved to Trask. Trask returned the wave but not the smile.

When the elevator doors slid open on the third floor, Jax was waiting for him.

"Did you enjoy your trip, my lord?" he asked, eyes blazing amid the white tattoo across his face.

"Very much, thank you, Jax."

"You have supplicants waiting for the brand, master."

Giles paused to glance at Jax, then scratched his head thoughtfully for a moment. "Let's move them to tomorrow night. I'm feeling a bit hungry, and thought I might go down for a bit of rejuvenation."

"I'll take care of it," Jax promised.

"Excellent," Giles replied.

He reached into his pocket for a ring that held keys to the Norton, a Jaguar he particularly liked, and a few others. As he walked down the hall to a different elevator, he spun the ring on his finger, the keys jangling loudly.

The elevator doors opened immediately when he pressed the button. Giles stepped in, selected the appropriate key, and inserted it. After he turned the key, he pressed the button marked "BB" and the elevator began to descend to the subbasement.

*A very interesting night,* he mused. Buffy's response had not been what he had hoped, but it had been precisely what he'd expected. He only dreamed that in time she would surrender to the conclusion that he was right, that she was meant to be a part of his regime. Still, it had been wonderful seeing her again. He had nearly been able to taste her blood even from across the room.

*A good night.*

Giles was humming as the doors slid open again.

Time for a visit with the god of bats.

Time to drink of power.

# CHAPTER 5

H*ome.*

*As Buffy opens her eyes her senses are suffused by the atmosphere of* home *that surrounds her. Soft jazz on the radio floats up to her along with the scent of something cooking.* Pancakes, *she thinks. Or not thinks exactly, so much as registers, 'cause thinking would require too much effort. Sunday morning, then, with pancakes and that jazz radio show that runs until noon.*

*The sheets smell fresh and clean and she burrows a little deeper under them, enjoying the feeling of the cotton against the side of her face. A strand of her hair is across her face and it tickles her nose so that she must blow it away with a puff of breath.*

*It's bliss, really, but somehow she cannot slip back into unconsciousness. Sleep has fled now and though she is warm and content, her mind has begun the day already without her cooperation. A bemused, drowsy grin steals across her face and, lazily, she opens her eyes.*

*It is bright outside her windows but there is no breeze. Her stuffed pig, Mr. Gordo, is a pink lump half hidden between her pillow and the headboard. Her alarm clock has numbers on it, but Buffy finds she cannot read them. She blinks several times, convinced it must be after nine o'clock because of the jazz. Then her vision seems to clear—though there wasn't anything wrong with it before—and the numbers on the alarm clock read "12:00." The numbers blink off and on like the clock on a new VCR.*

Power's out, *Buffy thinks. But she knows it can't be, because then where is the music coming from?*

*Her bliss ripples like the wind across the surface of a pond. With a sigh, she sits up in bed, and it is then that she notices the splash of purple on the wall. She recognizes it immediately, a carnival mask hand-painted in vivid colors. Her father brought it back from Venice for her when she was twelve years old.*

*During the move from L.A. to Sunnydale, it was shattered in the box. A box scrawled with the word* FRAGILE *on the top, bottom and on every side. Broken, this gift from her father, that he brought back specially for her from his business trip.*

*But here it is. Whole and unbroken.*

*Buffy is staring at it when her mother pops into the room, a bright smile on her face.*

*"You're up!" Joyce Summers says, her astonishment only half mockery. "The smell of pancakes luring you from bed?"*

*"Yeah," Buffy says slowly, but she is still troubled as her gaze returns to the purple and pink mask.* There's some red in it, too, *she notices for the first time.*

*Slowly, Buffy turns to focus on her mother. Joyce is almost bubbly. She loves Sunday mornings, the jazz and pancakes tradition, the time to share with her little girl who isn't so little anymore.*

*But now Joyce stares back at Buffy and the smile melts from her face as though it were a mask of ice, revealing an expression of despair beneath. She tries to hide the look, but cannot.*

*"Did I spill something on my blouse?" Joyce asks, picking at her shirt anxiously.*

*"Mom," Buffy begins.*

*"I should get back to the pancakes. They'll burn."*

*"Mom—"*

*"No!" Joyce snaps, panic flooding from her eyes. "Don't!"*

*"Mom—" Buffy's heart is breaking.*

*"Don't say it, Buffy!"*

*"You're dead, Mom."*

*Her mother's face goes slack and her arms drop to her sides as though all the energy, all the life, has been sucked from her. Drained from her. She shakes her head slowly, softly, and her words come out as a moan.*

*"Why did you have to say it?" Joyce Summers asks her daughter, weeping now. "It's Sunday morning."*

*Behind her, in the darkened hallway, Buffy sees another figure moving. Someone else in the house.*

Daddy? *she thinks. But that has to be just because of the mask, because her father isn't here. Doesn't live here. Never has. Never even calls anymore.*

*Then he steps into the room.*

*Giles.*

*Glasses on. Patient, knowing smile.*

*"Maybe you should go back to sleep now?" he suggests kindly. Paternally.*

*He takes Joyce in his arms and she collapses there, weeping, asking him why.*

*Buffy glances at the windows. The sun shines through, warm and bright. The wind had been dead before, but now a strong gust blows in and the carnival mask falls from its nail on the wall and shatters on the floor.* Tsking *in sympathy, Giles moves to pick up the pieces. When he reaches to touch the shards of her father—her father's* gift*—he slices his index finger.*

*He does not bleed.*

*"You're not dead," Buffy says to him, eyes welling with tears.*

*Giles glances up at her as though he has not quite heard.*

*Buffy narrows her gaze as she studies him, and she sees it then. The glasses and the benevolent gaze are a mask of ice, like the one her mother had worn.*

*"No," Giles agrees. "Not dead."*

*"But you should be," Buffy tells him.*

*And his face begins to melt, but now it is not ice melting. It is his flesh, peeling and blackening in the sun, running like wax. Still, there is no blood.*

*Another voice, off to her right, by the windows. "Buffy."*

*She turns toward the voice and sees Angel standing in front of an enormous pane of glass. Not her room. Not her windows. The shine burns through the window and silhouettes him and he stands with his arms out as though crucified, his eyes closed.*

*Buffy says his name. Angel opens his eyes and gazes down upon her, but he does not smile.*

*"He thinks like a vampire now. He doesn't understand love."*

*She realizes then that Angel's clothes hang heavily upon him because they are sodden with blood. It drips steadily from the edges of his jacket and the cuffs of his pants.*

*A noise by the door, and Buffy turns to see that her mother and Giles are gone. The room is dark now, no sun, no light, yet somehow she can just make out the shape of her door and the end of the bed.*

*Downstairs the music has died. The acrid odor of burning pancakes fills her nostrils and bile rises in the back of Buffy's throat. She closes her eyes against the darkness.*

Buffy woke with her head under the pillow, the stiff, starchy sheets wrapped around her legs. The smell of burned pancakes was still in her nose. She sat up quickly and swung her legs over the side of the bed, then rubbed her face vigorously with both hands as though she could erase the dream.

Her hands were dry.

Surprised, she glanced at her palms, then gently traced the skin under her eyes. No tears. And yet she was sure she was crying, had felt the tears welling in her, even subconsciously. When she woke she had known that if she opened her mouth it would be to sob.

But no tears.

Somehow she knew, then, that it was the younger Buffy in her, Buffy-at-nineteen, who was crying. But those tears never appeared on the cheeks of the woman whose body she inhabited. After all she had been through, Buffy-at-twenty-four was harder, more callous.

An image of Xander swam into her mind, and she understood that if it were not for the bizarre twinning of her soul, Buffy would have been like him. Without her younger self to temper the bitterness within her, she might have been just as numb and cold as he had become. As long as he had no hope, he had nothing to survive for. His despair might well get him killed.

*All or nothing,* Xander thought. The day had finally come when they would stop all this sitting around crap, saddle up, and head across the border. They would take Sunnydale back, kill Giles and every other leech that got in the way, or they wouldn't be coming back at all.

Which was just fine with him. Xander had been waiting for this day an awfully long time.

He had woken up hours before dawn, checked and double-checked his gear with only the light slipping under his door from the hallway to guide him, then suited up. When he knew there was nothing more that he could do, he popped *The Wild Bunch* into the DVD player and lay back on the bed. He didn't want to bother anyone else, so he left the sound off. Not that it mattered. He had seen the film dozens of times and knew most of the dialogue inside out.

*The Wild Bunch. The Outlaw Josey Wales. Once Upon a Time in the West. Red River. Stagecoach.* Nearly every DVD on the shelf was an old Western. He watched them over and over. Regular television was no distraction, for it was a joke to him to watch the news or even a sitcom, and think that the world on television was one that most people believed in.

They had no idea.

He might have read a novel, but he found that he had no patience for books anymore. His mind tended to wander into places he never wanted it to go.

On screen, the climactic battle erupted. Even without the volume, Xander could hear the gunshots. A bunch of men with no ties, nothing to lose, dying because they finally found something to stand up for.

A knock at the door. He glanced at the clock. 4:57 A.M. Xander slipped off the bed, grabbed his gear and opened the door. Oz stood in the corridor with Abel and Yancy. The werewolf was jittery, like he'd had too much caffeine, but over the years Xander had come to recognize that trait in him. He always got that way before a fight.

It was the animal in him.

"Time to roll," Oz said.

"Rolling," Xander replied.

Down the corridor, they met Buffy and Willow on the way down the stairs. All the other operatives were already outside, Xander knew. Or on the way out there. The grunts had been ordered to have everything prepared to move out at five A.M. precisely. But the group led by the Slayer was supposed to be different. Special. Ms. Haversham had handpicked this little squadron for the main event, the attack on Giles himself. So the rules that applied to everyone else didn't apply here.

*'Cause we've been doing it longer,* Xander thought. *Killing monsters. We're better at it 'cause we know how they think.*

Buffy hung back. "Xander. Got a minute?"

He glanced at her, then at Willow. She seemed surprised. Xander nodded toward Oz to let him know he and the others should go on, and when he went down the stairs, Willow went with him.

"Yeah?" he said, studying Buffy.

There was a kind of anger in her eyes that was not really anger. Something she wanted to say, maybe a lot. Xander had the feeling whatever it was, it wasn't anything he wanted to hear. For a moment he thought she was going to spill it, all the things that were on her mind.

Then whatever tension had built up in her seemed to subside. Buffy smiled, but there was no amusement in it.

"I wish I could bring that wall down," she said.

"What wall?"

"The one around you."

Then she reached up to grab him behind the head, stood on her tiptoes, and kissed him once, gently, on the lips. There was no romance in it, no passion, but he swallowed hard and forced himself not to look away.

"I love you, Xander," she said. "I did then and I do now. You still have people who care about you."

Her smile went away. Now her expression was grim, eyes dark. With the strength of the Chosen One, she gripped the back of his neck and shook him once.

"Don't die."

In the room that had once been the mayor's office, Giles sat across a small table from a Borgasi demon named Ace Tippette and sipped tea. Ace was not a tea drinker, but Giles had provided him with a glass of Kentucky bourbon. They had been in that room, across that table, long enough for the tea to get cold and the bourbon to get warm. The Borgasi seemed to wish he were elsewhere, but Giles would not relent. He gazed at the demon expectantly.

Ace ran a hand over the porcupine-like quills on his head and the back of his neck, and sighed for perhaps the thirteenth time. The black, wet nostrils that were about all he had for a nose twitched, and both sets of slitted eyes gazed about the room, avoiding Giles's face until at last he had no option but to respond.

"Ya gotta understand, the Borgasi ain't exactly a warlike race. I mean, all right, we understand the need to break kneecaps now and again, and we've buried our share of problems in the desert, but our clan has been living pretty peaceably alongside the humans in Vegas for, what, fifty, sixty years. Hell, they're most of our business these days. Since organized crime let us have a piece of things, Vegas runs smooth. Thanks to us, the place calmed down enough to become a freakin' tourist mecca, you know? We don't wanna mess up a good thing."

Giles nodded once, then took a sip of his tea. He grimaced at its temperature and set the cup down on the saucer. Contemplatively, he tapped a finger against the tip of his nose.

"You do seem to have quite a comfortable life out there in the desert, Ace. But let me suggest that perhaps you really aren't considering the larger picture here. You've seen a great deal of my operation on your visit tonight. I have revealed even more of it in some detail as I laid out the part I wish the Borgasi to play. Too much, I fear."

"Whoa, hold on there, chief. Nobody saw anything you didn't want them to see. We're here to parley, not to stick our noses in," Ace protested.

The vampire king smiled thinly. "Yes, well, putting that aside for the moment, let me see if I can cast this in a slightly different light for you. I'm expanding. Slowly, but quite inexorably, I assure you. I have one hurdle in my way. Much like walking a dog in Los Angeles, it is a mess I cannot avoid but am prepared to clean up after. I expect to have overcome that hurdle and have the detritus of its destruction cleared away within three or four days. After that time, I will continue to expand my sphere of influence. You could count on two hands the number of days before Los Angeles is in my hands. When I am done there, I will visit Las Vegas and I will take it."

Ace held up a hand, narrowing his gaze. "What the hell do you mean you're gonna 'take it'? You think we're just gonna clear out?"

A soft chuckle escaped Giles's lips. He did so enjoy Ace's company. "Perish the thought," he said as he steepled his fingers beneath his chin. "You *could* run, of course. Or I could destroy you all. But there is a third option I think we would both find preferable. As I complete my infiltration of Los Angeles, it would be simpler if, with your assistance, Las Vegas were already under my control. Simpler, and healthier, I think. For the Borgasi. After all, wouldn't you rather live as lords above the humans than as shadows among them?"

The vampire king had recently had the black paint scraped off one of the windows, and he could see that the sky was lightening outside, dawn sneaking in as if to catch the odd, errant night creature unaware. Now Giles offered a half-smile to the demon as he rose and went to close and latch the steel shutters that had been installed to block that single, clear window.

Giles turned and glanced at Ace again. "Put another way, my friend, wouldn't you rather live?"

For a second, he thought the Borgasi might snap. They weren't a warlike race, true, but they were dangerous when the spirit moved them. And proud, too. That was the real peril in baiting Ace, that Giles would tread too roughly on his pride. On the other hand, perhaps peril was not the right word, for Giles had laid out the future for the Borgasi in no uncertain terms. Despite his mannerisms and the absurdity of his nickname, Ace Tippette was not a stupid creature.

So Giles was not at all surprised when the demon shook his head and threw his hands up. "Not much use arguin' with that kinda logic, is there?"

"None," the vampire lord replied.

Ace stood and held out his hand. "All right, Giles. You give the orders, but you'll leave us alone to run things, yeah?"

Giles shook his hand firmly. "Agreed."

The Borgasi smiled, his hundreds of tiny, jagged teeth glistening damply. "Gotta say, it's gonna be interesting. Some of the boys got a problem with change. This'll throw 'em for a loop."

Ace paused and all four of his slitted eyes widened. "Say, when you get all the way to Atlantic City, you think we could have first dibs?"

"Dibs," Giles repeated. "By all means, Ace. By all means."

"Excellent." Ace shot him a thumbs-up.

The Borgasi turned to head for the door.

"One more thing," Giles said.

Wet nostrils sniffing the air as if sensing a change in the atmosphere of the room, Ace turned back to him.

"From now on, you will refer to me as 'my lord' or 'master.' Even 'majesty' is acceptable, though it always makes me feel a bit, oh, I don't know . . ." Giles tossed a hand in the air and grinned mischievously, ". . . self-conscious, I suppose."

Ace grinned back, misreading him. "You gotta be kiddin' me."

Giles glared balefully at him. "Decidedly not."

The quills on the Borgasi's head stood up slightly and he reached up to brush at them, forcing them to lay down again.

"Yeah, no, I mean . . . not a problem at all. You're the boss, right?"

"Not the boss," Giles replied. "The king."

There came a sudden rap at the door and then it was opened before Giles could even ask who it was. Jax glided into the room, practically crackling with anxiety.

Giles stared at him. "Jax," he said, the single word enough of an admonition to stop the servant in his tracks.

"Forgive me, my lord Giles," Jax said quickly, ducking his head in a rapid bow. "There's a, uh, a matter that's come up. An urgent matter."

Ace cleared his throat. "Know what? That's no problem. I'll just find my own way out, all right?" The Borgasi glanced anxiously at Giles. "We're at your service . . . my lord. Y'know, just buzz me when you want us to do it. We'll be ready."

Giles narrowed his eyes. "Excellent, Ace. I accept your mangled oath of fealty. Please wait in the corridor and Jax will escort you out momentarily."

The demon waved his hand in the air. "Nah, that's all—" He paused, glanced sheepishly back at Giles. "Right. I'll wait outside."

When Ace had left the room, Giles crossed his arms and glared expectantly at Jax. "What is it that couldn't wait?"

Jax glanced at the door and lowered his voice in almost theatrical fashion, apparently concerned that the demon would overhear.

"They're here, majesty. Five border sentries have called in to report a massive incursion along the southern border. As many as fifty to sixty vehicles thus far, separated into seven different groups at this count. Estimates have their individual numbers as high as three hundred."

"Excellent," Giles replied as he moved to the high-backed chair behind his desk. "A single-front battle. I had thought they would muster up enough operatives to attack from the north as well."

Jax stared at him. His expression was almost comical. "But, my lord, there are so many. We can only put a handful of your soldiers against them. There aren't more than twenty or thirty sunsuits."

"Oh, stop being such a mollycoddle, Jax. Granted, despite their vows of loyalty, most of the humans are unlikely to risk their lives to defend me, but some will. Enough to slow them down. And it isn't as though the demons I've been so careful to pamper are going to let their livelihoods be taken away. Under my rule, this is paradise for them. They can't afford not to help."

To his credit, Jax made an effort to quell his anxiety and stood a bit straighter. "Your orders, my lord."

Giles sighed. "We've planned for this eventuality,

Jax. Give the order. We'll see who obeys it. Losses are acceptable, even significant losses. But *loss* is not. I will be in the court in ten minutes. The battle will be conducted from there."

"Yes, my lord."

"Oh, and Jax? Make certain everyone is aware that the Slayer is mine. I want her captured if possible, but under no circumstances is she to be killed. Even if it means giving her safe passage to this building."

Now Jax dropped all pretense of calm and stared at him in horror. "But majesty, she'll ki—"

"No," Giles replied firmly. "She will not. I've seen it in her eyes now, felt it in her hesitation. She will do everything she can to stop me, but she will *not* kill me. That is the chink in her armor, Jax. She will be one of us before we see another dawn."

There were five vehicles in the phalanx that entered Sunnydale on the shore road, three Humvees and two troop carriers. There was a sense of urgency about the proceedings, but no one was in a hurry. They could not afford to be. Undercover operatives in Sunnydale had pinpointed at least a dozen major nests in town, and each team had been assigned two. They were to clean out the nests, taking out any opposition they met along the way, and thcn rcndczvous downtown to exterminate the opposition they were sure to encounter there.

Ms. Haversham had ordered that the nest in the Sunnydale Museum was to be left untouched for the moment, because the Council of Watchers could not abide the destruction of such valuable antiquities. When human control had been restored to the area, then the vampires in the museum would likely flee anyway. The older woman and her aides had established a command center at the Council building. From there they were in constant contact with the field units via headset communications systems.

One unit differed from the others, however, a small force whose mission was to proceed directly to City Hall. There they were to locate and destroy Rupert Giles, no matter the cost, eliminating any vampiric resistance they found along the way.

Buffy rode in the back of a troop carrier, engine rumbling loudly, rattling ominously. A castoff from the U.S. army, she suspected. But that was all right. They didn't need to go much farther. She glanced around her. Willow, Oz, Xander, and a dozen operatives handpicked by Ellen Haversham. Christopher Lonergan was in front, behind the wheel.

Just before their departure, Wesley had created a stir, protesting loudly to Haversham and Willow that he and Anna, the younger Slayer, were not part of this primary unit. There had been a lot of talk about the practical and effective dissemination of their forces, but Buffy didn't buy it for a second and she doubted Wesley did either.

The difference was that she suspected Wesley thought it was about him, that he was taking it personally. Buffy figured it had more to do with Haversham wanting to keep the Slayers separated to lessen the risk that they would *both* be killed today.

Up front, Lonergan cursed loudly and jammed on the brakes. The truck shuddered to a halt and Buffy held her breath.

"Abraxis demons. Four of them and a handful of humans," Lonergan explained.

Buffy glanced forward through the windshield and saw that they were in Docktown. A run-down tenement building ahead had been identified as a nest by Council spies. This was the moment when their smaller team was meant to break away from the phalanx, but there were yellow-skinned demons and some human collaborators in the way.

"Go," Buffy said.

Lonergan glanced at her in the rearview mirror. As a Council operative, he certainly had seniority in terms of years. But she was the Slayer, and the field leader of this mission.

"Beta team can handle this resistance," she pointed out. "That's what they're trained for, right? They'll firebomb that nest inside of ten minutes and be moving on. Let's go."

After only a moment's hesitation, Lonergan nodded. Gunfire erupted outside the truck and Buffy could hear the *whoosh* of flamethrowers as Lonergan accelerated, steering the groaning truck around the other vehicles and on toward the center of Sunnydale.

On toward City Hall.

The truck engine revved as they hit a straightaway. Out of the open back, she saw humans coming out of their homes and standing in the street to stare after the truck, and she wondered if they were relieved or terrified that help had finally come. If they even wanted help.

As Buffy glanced around at the operatives in the truck, one of the guys caught her eye. Yancy, she thought his name was. He was staring at Buffy as though she were a riddle he just could not unravel. The others were lost in their own thoughts, in preparation for the fight to come, and did not seem to notice Yancy's preoccupation with her. Even when Buffy stared back at him, the operative did not turn away.

"Can I help you with something?" she asked.

Yancy flinched, as though he had been unaware that he was staring. "Sorry," he said uncomfortably. "I was just thinking. I understand that you're the Slayer, and all, but this seems a bit kamikaze to me. The place will be well-guarded. They won't simply let us drive right in."

Buffy stared him down. "I think he will," she said. "Oh, he'll put up a fight, but I don't think he cares if we get in. That's the easy part. The way he talked to me the other night, I think he wants me to come."

"He *wants* you to kill him?" Yancy asked, incredulous.

"You're out of line, Yancy," Xander said curtly. "You don't have the first clue what the deal is here. It isn't your place to know. And it isn't your place to question. Buffy's got field command of this unit, and she knew what she was asking of us when she picked this team. You knew the risks when you agreed to be part of it. You want out, we'll stop the truck and you can walk back to base."

They all stared at Xander. Everyone except for Yancy, who had dropped his eyes and shifted his gaze away. Buffy smiled softly, silently thanking him. For the first time since she had come into this harsh world, she felt like they were all together again. It wasn't like it was, and it never would be. But they were together.

"I didn't mean anything by it," Yancy said.

"It's all right," Buffy told him. "It's a lot to ask anybody, to go on this mission."

"Trouble," Lonergan said abruptly. He gripped the wheel hard and hit the brakes.

Buffy swayed as the truck shuddered to a stop. She looked out through the front again and saw that there was a roadblock ahead. There were humans with assault weapons, and at least five vampires in protective gear.

"Fine," she said. "Trouble's just fine."

# CHAPTER 6

The sun gleamed off the vehicles parked across the road, and off each fold in the silver protective suits the vampires wore. Buffy crouched between the seats of the truck and stared through the windshield at them. The vampires weren't her concern, not when they were only lightly armed and the sun was up. The humans, though, the traitors who worked for them, they were going to be a problem.

"Buffy Summers!" a tall, bearded human shouted. "Come with us, right now, and everyone else in the truck gets to live. All we want is you."

"I'm all flattered," Buffy muttered.

There were nine humans that Buffy could count and at least six of them carried semiautomatic rifles. Assault weapons weren't something she was used to having to deal with. The forces of darkness tended to rely on more archaic weaponry, either out of a sense of style, an appreciation of antiques, or simply because they were too damn cocky to realize an Uzi was a more effective tool of destruction than a sword.

*Sword,* Buffy thought with a tiny smile flickering upon her lips. She reached under the bench in the back of the truck, just under where she had been sitting. Wrapped in a green blanket was the ancient, rune-engraved sword Giles had left for her. She had brought it along, wondering about it a great deal. Wondering if he had left it to give her an edge, or really, truly, as a gift. Or if, perhaps, there was something about the sword that was meant to hurt her. Some enchantment or curse. Some sort of trap.

Quickly, Buffy slipped a leather strap through the steel ring on the scabbard and then looped it over her shoulder, the sword lying across her back. Suddenly she was aware of eyes upon her. She glanced up to find everyone in the back of the truck staring at her. All of them, Willow, Xander, Oz, and the Council operatives, seemed coiled and ready to strike. The air crackled with the violence about to erupt, like the static electricity that hung in the sky just before a thunderstorm.

Through Lonergan's partially open window Buffy could hear music, a heavy-thumping blues-rock tune that filled the vacuum created by the tension between these two opposing forces.

The music was incongruous, and yet it wasn't.

In some ways, it was just what Buffy wanted, a sort of affirmation of the beating of her heart, the blood rushing through her. She glanced at Willow. "What can you give me for a diversion?"

As though their minds were cogs in the same machine, Willow scrambled into the midst of the troops, there in the back of the truck. On one knee, she glanced around at them.

"Buffy's going to walk right up to them," she told the others. "They will not attack her unless she draws the sword. They might try to make her disarm herself, but she won't."

Willow paused, glanced at Buffy. "Don't."

Buffy smiled. "Check."

"All right, then. Here's what we'll do . . ."

The music on the radio blaring from one of the cars in the roadblock had given way to screeching guitar from some seventies' rock band Buffy could not remember the name of. It ought to have seemed incongruous this early in the morning, less than an hour after sunup, but in light of the circumstances, there wasn't a lot that would have stood out as odd. As Buffy climbed out of the back of the truck, she could smell fire from somewhere not too far off. A vampire nest, she knew. Burning. The leeches dying, maybe wondering where Giles was when they needed him.

*No way,* she thought. *No way to make the world what it was. No way to ever make it right.* What Giles and his lackeys had done to southern California was akin to tearing a wound in the flesh of America. No way was this going to heal clean. But if they could cleanse the wound, purify it, then it *would* heal.

All that would be left behind were the scars.

Buffy picked up her pace, walked a little faster as she

went around the truck. A couple of the vampires swore when she appeared in their line of vision. One of them even took a few steps back. Before Giles took over, when this clan still answered to Camazotz, the demon-god kept the Slayer's existence a secret from them so that they would not be afraid. The Kakchiquels knew of her now, though. Giles had not taken that same precaution.

That was good. Their fear gave her an edge.

"Take the sword off and leave it on the pavement!" shouted the burly human who had called out before.

*The mouthpiece,* Buffy thought. The others might be there just because they thought that it was the safest way, the way to survive. Working for the vampires. But this guy, he clearly was into it. He was a part of the dark, rotten thing that had spread its filthy tentacles all through this town.

She kept walking.

All of the assault rifles swung around, their barrels aimed directly at her. Two of the human collaborators who had not yet shown weapons now pulled pistols. She thought she recognized one of them as a cop she had met once in Sunnydale. The other, though. She recognized him right off the bat.

*Parker.*

"Drop it, now, or we bring you to him dead," Mouthpiece shouted, a bit of panic tinging his voice.

If anything, her gait accelerated. Buffy strode toward them without the slightest hesitation. "I don't think so," she replied, close enough now that she barely needed to raise her voice. "He gave me this sword himself. It was a gift. I'm sure he wanted me to bring it when I came for a visit. And here I am."

Buffy ignored Mouthpiece as he struggled to figure out what to say next. The humans seemed more and more jittery as she closed in. The vampires moved slowly toward her as she approached. They were faceless behind the hoods they wore, and Buffy could imagine that there were no bodies in those silver suits, just the darkness, just the evil demon parasites that lurked in every vampire.

That's all they were, in the end, really. Corpse squatters. The image was gruesome, but it helped to think of Giles that way. *No, not Giles.* She wanted to stop herself from even thinking of the thing as Giles, but somehow she could not.

Maybe a dozen feet from the roadblock, Buffy stopped. The human collaborators—in front of the cars, behind them, standing on the hoods—seemed to hold their breath. Buffy saw Parker's eyes darting over toward Mouthpiece and then back to the sword that hung at her side. The vampires—*walking silver body bags*—encircled her like a pack of coyotes, exuding quiet malice, studying her, waiting for an opening.

"The sword," Mouthpiece said again, but this time his tone was uncertain. "On the ground."

Buffy smiled. With a small shrug of acceptance, she reached over her shoulder for the hilt of the weapon. The vampires twitched, drew back a step.

The tips of Buffy's fingers touched the sword.

The signal.

Buffy closed her eyes.

There was a burst of blinding light and searing heat that made her skin prickle. Screams of pain and alarm erupted all around her. Even with her eyes closed, she squinted harder against the brilliance of that light.

And she moved.

Etched upon her mind's eye, she could still see the vampires around her, the position each of them had stood in before Willow had cast this spell of illumination. Even in the daylight it was blinding, bright enough to sear the eyes of the humans, and even momentarily to stun the vampires despite the shaded face masks of their sunsuits.

With a sound like a bow across the strings of a violin, Buffy slid the sword from its scabbard. As it sliced the air she stepped forward and swung the blade. It connected, but was sharp enough that she felt only a small tug as one of the vampires was decapitated.

The sound was not unlike hearing someone close by biting into a crisp apple.

All around her, gunfire erupted. Buffy flinched, but only just barely. She had been prepared for it. Bullets tore the ground and she heard at least a few windows breaking around them. The human collaborators were firing, though they were all but blind in the glare of Willow's spell.

With their backs to the glare and their eyes squinted, the Council operatives could see well enough, and they began to fire back with far greater accuracy than their enemies. Someone cried out in pain and surprise. Buffy opened her eyes even as she spun and brought the sword across the neck of a second vampire. She squinted, and could barely see through her slitted eyes, but her instincts guided her well enough to make use of the advantage Willow had given them.

In all her time as the Slayer, she doubted she had ever moved so fast. One of them lunged at her; she brought the sword down as though she were chopping wood. Another had turned to run away from her; she sliced at it from behind, the silver protective hood staying on the head as it bounced off the ground, just before the entire creature turned to a small whirlwind of dust.

Only one remained. The vampire raised his weapon and fired two wild shots. She thought she could practically feel one of the bullets go by her head like a hornet. The cut from her sword was so fast, so clean, that for a second the head of the vampire remained on top of his shoulders. Then both head and body tumbled to the ground and disintegrated into embers.

Buffy slid the sword back into its scabbard. As she turned to face the collaborators, the Council operatives came up all around her. Willow and Oz and three others were on her left. Xander came up on her right with Yancy and a couple more. They seemed like little more than silhouettes in the bright glare of magickal light.

One of the operatives, a good-looking blond guy named Devine, took a bullet to the shoulder and went down hard. But the bullet had to be a stray, Buffy knew. The collaborators were firing blind, blinking rapidly as they tried to get their vision back. One of them stumbled off the roof of a car.

Backs still to the glare, the Council operatives rushed the roadblock and fired pistols, mostly to keep their enemies off guard. The idea was to disarm them without killing them.

Or it was, until Buffy saw a round red bullet hole appear in the center of Mouthpiece's forehead. He staggered back two steps, then fell against the passenger door of the car behind him with a *crump* of metal. He didn't move again.

"Hey!" Buffy snapped.

Beside her, Willow's hands worked quickly in the air. Even as Buffy watched, the Uzi in the hands of one of the humans turned to ice and shattered. The guy turned to run.

The power of the spell began to diminish and the brilliant, glaring illumination to fade back to normal daylight, but by then Buffy and her comrades had reached the roadblock. Even as she lashed out and cracked the jaw of a man in front of her, she saw Xander attacking and disarming a couple of others.

Willow had given them a vital advantage, allowing the confrontation to be dealt with quickly and without losing any of the members of their unit, but there was more to her than her skill as a sorceress. She was swift and graceful, a much better hand-to-hand fighter than she had been when they were younger, and she took the gun away from the man in front of her without him even really noticing he had lost it. To her left, Oz dove across the hood of a car and tackled a woman. But he was just Oz, not the wolf. Buffy had been clear about that. She wasn't sure the wolf could be trusted not to kill.

Someone *had* killed, though. Buffy glanced around, trying to figure out who it had been, and then she saw Yancy, a satisfied expression on his face. Before she could say anything, the human collaborators tried to grab her again. With a quick elbow, she cracked a nose, knocked someone unconscious. She spun around, and found Parker aiming a pistol at her from six feet away.

"You shouldn't have come back," Parker told her.

Hate and disgust filled Buffy then. He had always been a lowlife, but what he had become was worse.

"You don't think I can take that from you?" she asked him.

Parker smiled.

Then, from amid the chaos of the roadblock, Yancy appeared almost right beside Parker, and shot him in the side of the head.

"Yancy!" Buffy shouted as she watched Parker's corpse fall to the ground. "What the hell was that?"

The collaborators who weren't unconscious or dead took off running. A pair of Council operatives helped Devine to stand and began to examine the bullet wound in his shoulder.

Yancy holstered his weapon and the others began to crowd around, yet of all of them only Willow seemed even vaguely uncomfortable with what had happened.

Yancy gazed at Buffy expectantly. "He could have killed you. If you're the key to this thing working, we can't afford that. Not that I expected slobbery kisses, but a simple thank-you wouldn't have hurt."

Buffy glared at him. "You shot that other guy, too. The one who was doing their talking for them. Maybe you're just slow, but I meant what I said before. These are the people we're supposed to be trying to save. The only thing that matters here is that we get into City Hall, dust Giles, and, if we can manage it, get out alive."

Yancy's eyes grew stormy and his nostrils flared with anger. "Yeah? I'm sorry, I was under the impression that the people we were trying to save were the ones who weren't trying to kill us."

With that, he turned and marched back to the truck.

"Let's go," Buffy snapped at the others, and they all ran back to the truck.

"It did look like Parker had the drop on you," Willow whispered beside her.

"Not for a second," Buffy replied, though in truth she was not as certain as her tone implied.

She had not realized Xander was behind her, but now he jogged up next to her. "This isn't like it used to be, Buffy. Nobody *wants* anyone to get killed, but they've thrown in with the Big Evil; they know that's a risk. Maybe it's been conducted in secret until now, but this is a war. There have already been plenty of human casualties. The faster we end it, the fewer there will be in the future. Keep your head on straight, keep your eyes on the goal."

Difficult as it was for her, Buffy realized that Xander was right. Harsh, even callous perhaps, but right.

As they climbed into the back of the truck, Lonergan leaned around from the driver's seat and waited for instructions.

"You're supposed to be able to sense vampires, Christopher," Buffy said. "Try not to run us into any more. You see another roadblock, drive right through it. Just get us to City Hall."

As the truck rumbled on toward City Hall, Xander sat on the bench and glared at Tim Devine even as Hotchkiss cleaned and dressed the other man's bullet wound.

"You will stay with the vehicle, Devine. I'm not taking a liability into that building, and with that hole in you, that's exactly what you are," Xander told him, clipping off every word with his teeth.

He could feel the tension in the back of the truck and it pissed him off. Wasn't it bad enough, the pressure of what they were about to do? First Yancy squares off against the Slayer, and now Devine had to give him this crap. Out of the corner of his eye, he saw Buffy and Willow, side by side. Both of them seemed poised to speak up, take some action, and he shot them a quick, sidelong glance to let them know he would handle it. Buffy might be field commander, with Willow running a close second, but Xander and Lonergan were the ones who were really responsible for these grunts. Xander was not about to let the operatives in his unit forget that.

Devine grimaced as Hotchkiss wrapped the bandages tighter across his shoulder. Then he narrowed his gaze and stared at Xander. "Don't get up in my face, Harris," Devine said. "The coagulant stopped me from bleeding too much. I'm right-handed, which means I can still fire my weapon. And you are *not* running this mission."

With a soft chuckle, Xander shook his head. The Council had worked with the U.S. government to develop a chemical treatment that acted as a coagulant upon their blood when it was exposed to air. The army had recently begun to use the same treatment. If they were wounded, it caused the bleeding to stop quickly. It also made it decidedly unpleasant for a vampire to drink from them. Devine was right about that, but it didn't change his mind.

"First of all, it's *Mis*-ter Harris to you, Devine. I may not be your direct commander, but I am your superior on this mission. Do you hear anyone in this truck contradicting me? What it comes down to is this: you are wounded, and therefore at least partially impaired. You are not one hundred percent. Could cost your life, but that's your risk. The thing is, you're in there covering somebody's flank, they are trained to be able to rely on you. If they can't, you're a liability.

"You stay in the truck."

Devine practically snarled in response, but Xander held firm. A second later the truck's brakes squeaked and it rattled to a stop.

"We're here," Lonergan said from the front. He touched the headset he wore and listened for a moment. "From the sound of things, all the other units have reached their initial targets and have started to exterminate the nests. At this point, even best case scenario, Giles either knows we're coming or knows we're here."

Xander glanced over at Buffy and Willow. "Drive by?" he asked.

The two women looked at each other, and in that moment, memories flooded through him of his childhood with Willow, and of the way things had changed after Buffy had come into their lives. Things had been so simple once upon a time, even after they had discovered what really lurked in the shadows of the world. They had been teenagers, then, tangled in emotions and hormones and a belief that they could keep the monsters at bay.

They had failed.

But now, looking at the women his friends had become, at cool, confident Willow with her red hair tied back in an oh-so-serious ponytail, and at edgy, wiry Buffy, her features somehow more beautiful despite the ghosts that seemed to haunt her eyes . . . now Xander believed that it was possible for them to win.

And he was not going to compromise that hope for anyone.

Willow nodded to Buffy.

"We're doing the drive-by, Christopher," Buffy told Lonergan.

"Done," the man replied.

Lonergan put the truck in gear again and floored it. Xander turned to Alex Hotchkiss, an operative he'd trained with when the Council had first set up shop for real in California, and held out his hand.

"Let's knock," he said.

Hotchkiss grinned, then reached under the bench and produced a long plastic cylinder. He uncapped one end and slid out a 66mm M72-A7 disposable antitank weapon. What always amazed Xander about these things was that they looked harmless enough, more like a fat telescope than anything else. Hotchkiss handed it to him and Xander slipped the strap over his shoulder. He sat on the floor of the truck with his back braced against one bench and his feet steady on the floor.

"Five seconds," Lonergan warned. He spoke quickly into the headset to the drivers of the other trucks that were rolling in even now to back them up.

"Gimme a window," Xander snapped.

Yancy and another operative, Darren Abel, scrambled to unhook a set of latches on the wall of the truck. They bracketed—and held in place—a four foot square section of the sidewall. Behind Xander, Buffy and Willow undid a matching set on the other wall. When the latches were open, Hotchkiss shot Xander a look.

"Ready!" Xander shouted.

"Go," Lonergan replied, barely a second later.

The two operatives shoved the unlatched section of wall and it swung out and down, even as Buffy and Willow did the same on the other side. They leaped out of the way. Xander saw guards running toward their transport and the two other trucks that were rolling in. A pair of Draxhall demons lumbered menacingly in front of the doors to City Hall. Xander peered through the M72's sight, saw the elegant granite steps in front of the building, aimed at the Draxhall demons and the huge double doors right in the center of the building's face, and fired.

The four-pound missile roared out of the M72's fat barrel with a hiss like God opening a God-size can of soda after the Devil shook it up. The backfire roared flames out the rear of the barrel through the opening behind him. Xander slammed against the bench and he knew his back would be badly bruised from the force of it.

The front doors of City Hall exploded, shattering the stone frame around them and ripping the Draxhall demons to shreds.

Lonergan kept driving, but he cut the wheel, turning the truck in a hard circle to bring it back around toward the front. Operatives fired their weapons through the now open ports in the truck's walls, and out the back. Several human sentries went down, but the others turned to run.

Xander glanced at Buffy. "Couldn't be helped," he told her. "But at least the others are running."

She nodded grimly.

Then the truck slammed to a stop again.

"Go! Go!" Willow shouted. "Stay together."

They leaped out through the openings in the wall, and through the back, hustling as fast as they could. The other vehicles were also disgorging their troops. At the rear of the truck, Xander turned and shot a last look at Tim Devine.

"Get behind the wheel. Don't let them take the truck. If any of us lives through this, we'll need a ride home."

Devine, resigned to being left behind, nodded grimly.

The sword banged against Buffy's back as she ran up the granite steps. It had worked so well that she was tempted to use it now, but in close quarters with the rest of her team, she did not want to risk it, so instead she clutched a stake in her hand as they ran through the debris of the ruined doors. Then they were inside, leaping over large chunks of stone and shattered wood.

Buffy blinked, her eyes adjusting, and then she saw them. At least twenty vampires were gathered in the huge foyer, and more were scrambling down the stairs and running along distant corridors to join them, to save their master, their king.

Around her, she glimpsed Xander, Willow and Oz, Christopher Lonergan, Yancy and Abel, Hotchkiss and the other members of the squad. More were pouring in behind them. There was a sort of pause, just a tiny moment where time seemed to be suspended, where no one moved.

Buffy glanced at Willow.

"Oz," Willow said.

In an instant of howled pain, Oz transformed. Then the moment broke and the vampires rushed forward and the fight began. The operatives were in close quarters battle. No rifles or assault weapons here. There were crossbows and shotguns and some pistols, and there were stakes.

Oz leaped into the fray first, slashing at two of the vampires before driving one down to the ground and ripping its throat out with a single thrust of his enormous jaws. Buffy cringed when she saw it, for she had a sense that Oz hated what he was. He would use it to help make things right, use it maybe just because Willow asked him and she still had a hold on his heart, but he hated it. Buffy could see why.

Then she was in the thick of things and had no more time for thought. A high side kick drove one of them back, a quick elbow cleared the way, then she staked two in quick succession. Long, filthy claws raked at her back and she dusted a third without even glancing back at it, instinct alone helping her locate its heart.

Around her, the fight raged, dark and savage and throwing dust all about. It clogged Buffy's throat and nostrils and she nearly vomited on the floor as she realized she was breathing vampires.

Yancy died, screaming as a pair of vampires tore into him . . . the scream cut off abruptly when one of them broke his neck. Then Xander was there, dusting Yancy's killers, grim and silent. He wore a crossbow slung over his shoulder on a strap, but for the moment he was using a stake. He liked to get close to them, he had said, to make sure the job got done.

But still the vampires came. There were just too many of them, a building filled with them.

Of course, that was exactly what they had expected.

"Now?" Willow asked.

"Do it," Buffy replied.

With a wave of her hands and a shout in some ancient tongue Buffy could not even identify, Willow cast a spell that set half a dozen vampires near her ablaze. The fire roared up from them and reached the ceiling, and then the ceiling itself started to burn. Fire licked across the wood, raced as if alive to the edges of the ceiling and began to incinerate the walls as well. It was unnaturally fast, a ravenous flame. It was exactly what they wanted.

The vampires continued to fight, but tried to shy away from the fire. They began to cluster near the middle of the room.

As if on cue, the emergency sprinkler system in City Hall turned on, spraying hundreds of jets of water down upon them, just in the massive foyer alone.

Some of the vampires had begun to look frightened of the flames, but now those same leeches laughed and smiled, and the menace came back into their faces. Orange electric fire burned in their eyes, like distant stars in the black abyss of the tattoos they all had across their faces. Once it had been the symbol of Camazotz, but no one knew what had become of the god of bats. Now, though, that symbol was the brand of Giles.

Bloodlust filled the vampires. Power crackled all through them as the water doused the flames. They knew their numbers were greater, knew that they would triumph eventually.

Which was when Christopher Lonergan stepped forward, a crucifix raised in his hand, and began to recite a prayer in Latin. He blessed the water that fell from the sprinklers above.

Blessed it, and made it holy.

Christopher Lonergan was a priest.

The holy water burned the vampires, their skin steaming. They started to scream. All the bravado and power that had been in them a moment ago evaporated and they looked almost foolish with the tattoos across their faces, like children at Halloween.

Some of them tried to run, but the operatives moved in. The vampires shrieked with agony from the water that fell even as Buffy and the rest of the team began to eliminate them, to scythe through them like a field of wheat.

It was a massacre after that.

In that moment, the reason for this attack hit Buffy hard. *Giles,* she thought. In her mind's eye she saw him, a thousand shards of memory, images of him with Jenny Calendar, or in battle, or standing up to the bullying of Quentin Travers. She thought of Giles with his nose stuck in a book, face scrunched up in contemplation, of the glances of half-feigned shock or disapproval he so often shot at Xander or even Buffy herself, and of the way that he had always been able to comfort her, sometimes even without saying a word.

Somewhere in this building, the evil that had usurped her mentor's body lurked, waiting. She had no doubt that the thing that Giles had become would find a way to shield himself from the holy water. But she also knew that it would not run. It wanted her to find it, to find him. It wanted to face her. The very feelings and memories that filled her now, those were the things that Giles relied upon to throw her off-balance.

Buffy spotted Willow and Oz, still a wolf, not far away. She ran to her friend. Oz turned with a snarl, then sniffed at Buffy and was calm.

"Let's go," the Slayer said. "Let's find him now. I want this done with. We'll start in the basement. No windows, so he'd think that was the safest place for him. If I'm wrong, we'll work our way up from there."

Willow nodded, turned to beckon for Xander to come with them.

Then Buffy shouted to Lonergan. "You've got command! Scour the place. Don't leave any of them. We're starting in the basement and we'll catch up when we can."

Lonergan gave her a wave and Buffy nodded in satisfaction as Xander ran over to join them.

"All right. Let's go," she said, then led the way down the corridor toward the stairwell that would take them to the basement.

It was just the four of them—Buffy, Willow, Xander, and Oz—but that was okay. Once upon a time, she could remember having thought that in order for her to be an effective Slayer, she had to learn to operate on her own. But now she realized how foolish that was. *This is the way it's supposed to be. This is right.* The same way that Xander had insisted Devine stay behind, so that no one had to count on someone who might not live up to expectations, that was how she felt now.

She knew she could count on her friends to back her up, no matter what, and no matter how long it had been since they had been in the midst of such anarchy together.

They passed right by the elevator banks. With the fire alarms blaring and the sprinkler system on, chances were the elevators would have opened on the nearest floor and then frozen in keeping with safety regulations.

A red EXIT sign ahead marked the door that led to the basement. Buffy didn't even bother trying the knob. She popped a side kick at the metal door, right beside the knob. Metal shrieked and tore and it banged open.

Buffy led them onto the landing, out of the shower of water from the sprinklers. The stairs were unattractive, concrete and metal. A three-foot number one was painted on the wall. With a quick glance upward, Buffy started down toward the basement. Oz followed right after her, sniffing the air and the stairs as they went. Willow was behind him, and Xander covered their flank. He had the crossbow dangling from a leather strap around his shoulder like a rock star with his favorite guitar, but he let it hang there as he pulled a nine millimeter Glock from its holster at his side.

Not a word was spoken as they descended.

At the bottom of the stairs was another door. A huge letter *B* was painted on the wall, but other than that there were no markings. No guards. Nothing out of the ordinary at all. Buffy paused on the last step, feeling the damp heat of the werewolf's panting breath on her back. Oz sniffed the air several times in quick succession and began to growl low.

Buffy nodded. "I smell it, too," she said.

"What?" Willow asked.

"Don't even know what to call it," Buffy told her. "Static. Like the bug zapper in Xander's backyard."

"Electricity," Willow said, her voice a sort of hush.

"Exactly."

Willow stepped past Oz. Buffy noticed the sorceress's

hand stroking the werewolf's neck gently as she went by him. Willow studied the door for a moment, then glanced over her shoulder at Xander.

"I'm a little tired already," she told him. "Catch me if I fall."

"Always," Xander replied without emotion. It was a simple statement of fact.

"Hey," Buffy said. "I can do it if it's too much—"

"No," Willow said quickly. "We need you in front. Just be ready."

A small smile flickered on Buffy's features. "No such thing. But let's do it anyway."

Willow took a deep breath, sketched in the air with her hands, muttered perhaps four words in what sounded like Greek. Buffy felt a wave of absolute, bone-chilling cold push past her, and she shivered.

The door turned to ice and there was a crackle and pop as the electricity running into and around it shorted out. Willow swayed slightly, but her arm shot out and she leaned against the wall. Buffy grabbed her arm and Xander moved in from behind, but she shook it off after a moment. They were on the landing at the bottom of the stairs now, and Oz moved around them, closer to the door. The werewolf's growling grew louder and more menacing.

"Oz," Buffy said.

The wolf turned, black lips curled back from gleaming teeth. She saw no human intelligence in his eyes, but she knew that he at least partially understood what went on around him.

"Giles is mine," she said.

Then Buffy glanced back at Xander and Willow. Without another word, they both nodded. She took a deep breath, faced the frozen door again, then leaped at it in a high drop kick. The ice shattered into a million tiny shards. The door was gone. They were in.

The basement was dark save for the amber glow of emergency lights on the walls. It was practically a dungeon; not fit for a king. Clearly this was not Giles's lair. There were other corridors that led to this place, other doors on the other side of the vast chamber in the basement, but this was the main room. Once it had undoubtedly been a massive storage area of some kind.

In some ways, it still was.

Half a dozen Kakchiquel sentries, their eyes blazing orange in the darkened room, moved to attack them. But the sentries could not keep them from seeing what lay in the basement.

Bats hung from the pipes that ran all across the ceiling. On the floor beneath them, shackled and chained to iron rungs sunk deep into the concrete, was the god of bats, the demon Camazotz. His green, pocked flesh was obscenely bloated, like a leech that had feasted until it was ready to explode. The demon-god's withered wings were barely visible underneath its grotesque bulk. There were sores on its flesh. Its wide eyes were milky white. Blind. Its tongue slithered over its needle teeth and dry, cracked lips.

Yet Camazotz himself was not the thing that horrified

Buffy the most. For around the swollen, distended demon, seven vampires were latched onto his putrid flesh, sucking at him like newborn kittens, crackling with the energy they siphoned from the captive demon's blood.

Buffy shuddered, stomach convulsing at the sight.

"Now *that* is really gross."

At the sound of her voice, the suckling vampires glanced up, mouths smeared with demon blood. The sentries surrounded them. Camazotz began to cry out in a high, keening, lonely wail that sent a chill through her. *The god of bats,* she thought, *has gone insane.*

And Giles was nowhere to be found.

. . . TO BE CONTINUED

# About the Author

CHRISTOPHER GOLDEN is the award-winning, *L.A. Times*–bestselling author of such novels as *Straight on 'til Morning, Strangewood, Prowlers,* and the *Body of Evidence* series of teen thrillers, which was honored with an award from the American Library Association as one of its Best Books for Young Readers.

Golden has also written or co-written a great many books and comic books related to the TV series *Buffy the Vampire Slayer* and *Angel,* as well as the script for the *Buffy the Vampire Slayer* video game for Microsoft Xbox. His other comic book work includes stories featuring such characters as Batman, Wolverine, Spider-Man, The Crow, and Hellboy, among many others.

As a pop culture journalist, he was the editor of the Bram Stoker Award–winning book of criticism *CUT!: Horror Writers on Horror Film,* and co-author of both *Buffy the Vampire Slayer: The Monster Book* and *The Stephen King Universe.*

Golden was born and raised in Massachusetts, where he still lives with his family. He graduated from Tufts University. He is currently at work on the fourth book in the *Prowlers* series, *Wild Things,* and has recently completed a new novel for Signet called *The Ferryman.* There are more than six million copies of his books in print. Please visit him at www.christophergolden.com.

POCKET
PULSE